THE BILLIONAIRE'S HEART

THE SHERBROOKES OF NEWPORT BOOK 12

CHRISTINA TETREAULT

The Billionaire's Heart, ©2018 by Christina Tetreault
Published by Christina Tetreault
Cover Designer: Amanda Walker
Photographer: JW Photography
Cover Model: Daniel Rengering
Cover Model: Kristen Lazarus
Editing: Hot Tree Editing

PROLOGUE

April Fools Day

LEAH PAUSED at the sound of her ringing cell phone and fished the device from her purse. Before answering she checked the caller ID, because after the day of travel she'd experienced, there was only a handful of people she was willing to talk to. Her cousin Courtney's name was displayed across the screen. A call from Courtney or anyone else in her family, she'd take.

"Hey," Leah greeted, entering the luxury condo building when the doorman opened the door for her.

Courtney didn't give her a chance to say anything else. "Did you know?"

"I know a lot of things. You'll need to be more specific, Court." Since she was in no rush and Harry wasn't even expecting her tonight, Leah crossed the building's main lobby to one of the leather sofas rather than continue to the elevators.

"Right, sorry. Did you know your brother is C.S. Hilton? I didn't find out until this afternoon. Curt stopped by my mom's house to wish her a happy birthday, and he mentioned it."

Shoot. She'd reminded herself yesterday to call Aunt Marilyn today and wish her a happy birthday. After the delays at the airport caused by the weather and then the awful plane ride, it had completely slipped her mind.

"Yes, I knew. Curt told me not long after *Fatal Deception* came out." When he had confided in her, her reaction had been first shock, followed by amazement and pride because it had been a fabulous novel. In fact, she couldn't remember the last time she'd been so eager for an author to release a second book. Unfortunately, the last time she asked Curt about it, he hadn't even finished writing the next one.

"I can't believe you didn't tell me. We even talked about the book after we both finished it."

Leah remembered well. More than once she'd almost blurted out the truth during their conversation. "I wanted to tell you, but it wasn't my secret to share. And Curt didn't want too many people to know. Not even family."

"Fair enough, but I still can't believe Curt wrote it," Courtney replied. "Did you also know he left Nichols Investment?"

Leah's jaw all but fell into her lap. She along with everyone else in the family knew Jim Burke, the current CEO of the Boston-based investment firm, was grooming Curt to take over for him at some point in the near future. "He did?"

"Yep. He told us that at least for the foreseeable future he plans to do nothing but work on his next novel and remodel the house he bought."

Another fixer-up? This had to be at least his fourth. She'd expected Curt's interest in renovating old homes to have dwindled by now. If he'd not only bought another one but also left the firm so he could dedicate more time to working on it, it was the opposite.

"He plans on living in it too while he does the work," Courtney continued. "The house is somewhere up in New Hampshire. I forget the name of the town, but he said it's just over the Massachusetts border."

Obviously her big brother had been inhaling too many paint fumes while doing all these renovations. She'd have to call him later and try to set him straight. He had a gorgeous place in Boston and a house right on the beach in Newport. He didn't need to live in a run-down house in New Hampshire, no matter how much he enjoyed doing his renovation projects.

"Anyway, I'm heading out to Greenwich to visit Callie and Dylan this weekend. Do you want to meet in the city Sunday and do some shopping?" Courtney asked, referring to their cousin and her husband.

Anyone who'd ever seen the inside of Leah's closet knew there weren't too many things she loved more than a good shopping spree, especially if she had company while she did it. And with the exception of maybe Paris, there was no better place to shop than New York City in her opinion. Even Los Angeles paled in comparison.

"I've been in California all week for work, and before that I was in Utah for three days. I just got back today. Let me make sure Harry doesn't have any plans made for us this weekend, and I'll get back to you."

"Sounds good. Talk to you soon."

Rather than toss her phone back in her purse, Leah pulled up Aunt Marilyn's contact information. When she didn't answer, Leah left a message wishing her a happy birthday and promising to call again soon.

"Hey, stranger," a male voice she recognized well greeted. "Where have you been?"

Zipping her purse closed, Leah smiled up at Gavin Kincaid, Harry's half brother. She'd first met him about a year ago at a fundraiser, but over the past two and a half months she'd gotten to know him well, since Harry and Gavin were currently sharing one of the building's luxury condos while Harry's new home was being built. Although how they managed to coexist in the same space, she didn't know. They seemed to be polar opposites. They didn't even share a family resemblance. While Harry was tall and lanky with blond hair and hazel eyes, Gavin had dark hair and dark eyes like their father. And the word lanky wasn't an adjective anyone would associate with Gavin. At perhaps a little over six feet tall, he had a build perfectly suited for doing underwear ads.

"First Utah and then California. I just got back today." Leah gestured toward the suitcase Gavin held. "Looks like I'm not the only one who has been traveling. Business or pleasure?"

"People travel for pleasure?" Gavin asked, feigning a shocked expression.

"Occasionally. You should give it a try sometime."

Unlike her boyfriend, who did the absolute minimum at the office, Gavin was the stereotypical workaholic. In fact she'd only met one person worse than him: longtime family friend Dylan Talbot, before he met and married her cousin Callie.

"I'll keep it in mind. Are you heading upstairs or are you on your way out?" He tipped his head in the direction of the elevators.

Standing, Leah smoothed down her skirt and slipped the purse straps over her shoulder. "Heading up. I wasn't supposed to be back until tomorrow morning, but I wrapped things up in California and caught an earlier flight home. I thought I'd surprise Harry tonight. Assuming he's home, anyway."

Gavin pretended to check his wristwatch. "Well, it's after six, so we both know he won't be at the office. But if he's not home, you're welcome to hang around until he gets back."

They kept up a steady conversation as they crossed the lobby to the elevators, and not for the first time she wondered why Gavin remained single. He was easy to talk to and even easier on the eyes. Actually, the only major flaw he seemed to have was that he worked too much. As far as flaws went, it wasn't the worst one a person could have. Given the right incentive, it was also one a person could overcome. She'd witnessed that firsthand.

"Will you be traveling again soon?" Leah asked, exiting the elevator when the doors opened. Perhaps it was time she took a page out of her best friend's handbook and tried her hand at matchmaking. A man like Gavin deserved to have someone special in his life, and she had plenty of female friends and relatives to pick from.

Gavin unlocked the door and turned the handle. "I have no plans to go anywhere right now, but we both know things come up." He pushed the door open and allowed her to enter first. "What about you?"

Leah made a mental note to review her list of single friends and relatives soon. If Tory, her cousin, could play Cupid, so could she. "Thankfully, I won't be going anywhere either." While she loved traveling, she hated doing it for work. "Unless it involves a trip to a sandy beach with a fruity —" At the sight of the wedge sandals near the leather sofa, her lips froze. Unless Harry had decided to give ladies' footwear a try, a woman was visiting him, because those were not her shoes.

Don't jump to any conclusions. Harry did have two half

sisters, although judging by the size of the sandals, they couldn't belong to Piper. She was only ten years old and, although tall for her age, there was no way those sandals belonged to her.

That doesn't rule out Vivian, she reminded herself. Doubt settled in because she couldn't imagine Vivian visiting Harry; while they were half siblings, she got the impression the two didn't get along well.

"On a beach with a fruity what?" Gavin's question suggested he'd either not noticed the feminine footwear or knew who the shoes belonged to.

Before she could answer his question or pose one, the owner of the sandals called out from across the condo, "Hey, Harry, where do you keep the bottle opener?" The woman's voice contained a lyrical southern accent.

Definitely not Vivian. She'd met Gavin's twin sister. Like Harry and Gavin, she'd grown up in New England and sounded nothing like the woman searching for a bottle opener in the kitchen.

"Should be in the top drawer next to the wine fridge." Harry's voice came from the direction of the bedrooms.

Harry's visitor came into view carrying a bottle of wine and dressed in a New England Rebels T-shirt—a shirt Leah had seen Harry wear—and nothing else. When she realized Gavin and Leah were standing there, she stopped and smiled.

Taking in a deep breath, Leah counted to ten and resisted the urge to stomp out like a child. She'd known going into their relationship that Harry had dated a lot of women. She hadn't held it against him. She'd had a fair number of boyfriends herself. However, she'd assumed that despite his long list of past girlfriends, he'd be faithful. The redheaded bombshell standing a few feet away showed just how wrong she'd been.

Idiot.

"Hi, Gavin," the redhead greeted.

Why it bothered her that Gavin knew the half-dressed woman standing in front of them she couldn't say, but it did.

A lot.

Curious to see how'd he react, Leah shot a look in his direction.

Either he's a fabulous actor, or he really doesn't recognize her.

"We met in the elevator last month," the redhead continued when Gavin didn't reply. "You had a suitcase with you and mentioned you were flying out for business."

"Still can't find it, Amy?" Harry entered the living room before Gavin confirmed he remembered the encounter. Unlike his female guest, he wore jeans but no shirt.

Something between shock and concern crossed Harry's face as he came to an abrupt stop. "Leah, I thought you weren't getting back until tomorrow."

Various curses passed through her mind, but rather than call him every vile name ever invented to describe two-timing jerks, she tilted her head in Amy's direction. "I can see that."

Without waiting to hear whatever response or excuse Harry might come up with, she turned on her heel and walked out.

If Amy wants you, she can have you.

LATER HE'D GIVE Harry a piece of his mind, but first he wanted to make sure the woman his brother had just betrayed was okay. After giving his half brother a dirty look, Gavin bolted out the door.

"Leah, wait," he called as she pressed the button for the elevator. "Are you all right?"

She turned and faced him, a forced smile if he'd ever seen one painted on her face, but at least she wasn't crying. He never knew exactly how to handle crying women.

"Peachy."

"I'm serious. What Harry—"

Behind her the elevator doors opened. "Really, I'll be fine, Gavin, but thanks for asking. And while finding out like this stinks, it's better I learn what a jerk Harry is now before I waste any more time on him."

Half brother or not, Gavin could've told her the day she walked into his condo what an asshole Harry was when it came to women and relationships. No doubt about it, the guy was following in their father's footsteps. The only real difference between them was that Donald Kincaid cheated on both his wives and girlfriends while Harry had been wise enough to keep away from the altar.

"Have a nice weekend. And don't forget to try taking a vacation sometime. I think you work too much." She stepped inside the elevator and gave him a little wave. "See you later, Gavin."

The doors closed before he could offer up a reply. Crossing the hall, he entered the condo in time to hear Amy call his half brother a dirtbag. An appropriate if tame name for Harry. Soon after she stormed across the living room dressed in her own clothes.

"Amy, c'mon, wait a minute. I can explain," Harry called, following her into the room still only wearing his jeans.

After grabbing her sandals, she continued toward the door without even stopping to put them on. "Yeah, I bet you can," Amy tossed over her shoulder before opening the door and walking out.

"Damn it." Harry raked a hand through his already disheveled blond hair. "I need a drink. Do you want one?"

"*You* need a drink?" Gavin advanced on his half brother,

his hands clenched into fists. He never resorted to violence, but damn he wanted to punch Harry. "Your girlfriend just walked in on you with another woman, and you're the one who needs a drink? How the hell do you think Leah feels?"

With a shrug, Harry entered the kitchen and went straight for the fridge.

Pain shot through Gavin's cheek, and he relaxed his jaw as he stormed into the room. "If you feel a great need to take after Dad in some way, try emulating his boardroom skills instead." Their father had a lot of faults, but he knew how to run a successful multimillion-dollar business.

"Who do think encouraged me to stay with Leah this long anyway?" Harry opened a beer and took a swig. "If it'd been up to me, I would've dumped her weeks ago. She might be pretty, but she's a prude. Why do you think I've been hooking up with Amy or Satin whenever Leah's not around?"

He'd known Harry was lazy but hadn't realized he was stupid too. Gavin had been attracted to Leah Sherbrooke from the moment he met her at a Clean Water Matters fundraiser a year ago. Unfortunately, at the time she'd been involved with someone. When Harry showed up at the condo they were temporarily sharing back in January with her on his arm, Gavin couldn't believe his rotten luck. If he had known Leah was single, he would've reached out to her long before her cousin Tory introduced her to Harry.

Despite her being with his half brother, Gavin's attraction hadn't disappeared. In fact it had grown over the past two and a half months. Thanks to all the time she'd spent at the condo, he'd gotten to know her as a person rather than just another member of the wealthy and powerful Sherbrooke family.

"Dad wanted you to stay with her?" As far as he knew, their father had never cared whom any of his children got involved with.

"Yeah. Since we were together, he expected to finally

have a connection to the Sherbrooke family so he could get Culloden restaurants into their hotels."

At times like this, Gavin wondered how it was possible Donald Kincaid was his father.

"He's going to be pissed when he finds out we're no longer together." Harry swallowed another mouthful of beer. "Do me a favor and don't say anything to him. I'm not in the mood for one of his *friendly* chats."

Gavin had been on the receiving end of Dad's chats, and he knew there was nothing friendly about them. All things considered, he couldn't think of anyone more deserving of one than Harry, but he was a little old to be tattling on his younger brother.

"I'll leave the honors to you. But let me know when you plan on giving him the news, so I can turn off my phone."

Since they were living together, Dad would find some way of placing part of the blame on his head—as if he'd ever been able to influence Harry's decisions. Regardless, ever since they'd been kids, whenever Harry screwed up, Dad found a way to transfer some of the responsibility onto Gavin's shoulders. Maybe if Dad had forced Harry to deal with things more, the guy would be more of a responsible adult today.

"Hopefully I can convince Leah to give me a second chance and keep Dad off my ass." Harry opened the fridge and pulled out a pizza box. "I'll give her a few days to cool off and then stop by her house."

His half brother had a better chance of reaching the top of Mount Everest naked in the middle of a blizzard than of convincing Leah to take him back. Other women might fall for Harry's promises, but not her. Unlike a lot of the women Harry dated, Leah had a brain in her head.

"Good luck with that," Gavin called out as he walked past Harry. *And thank you*, he silently added.

As much as he hated the reason why Leah had dumped his half brother, with Harry and Leah's relationship over, it meant he could now do what he'd wanted to do since he first met her. Ask out Leah Sherbrooke.

ONE

Three Months Later

"DID you know it was going to rain today?" Leah paused at the entrance to the country club's restaurant.

Like she often did, she'd met Gavin at Pine Ridge for a friendly round of golf followed by a late dinner. They hadn't even made it out to the first tee when the rain started. She may enjoy golf but by no means did she enjoy it enough to play in the rain. Thankfully, they managed to get back to the clubhouse before the true downpour started, so while she'd gotten a little wet, it didn't appear as though she'd taken a shower in her clothes.

Gavin shook his head and held open the door for her. "Last I checked the storm wasn't supposed to start until much later this evening." A crack of thunder rumbled outside, and then a bolt of lightning lit up the suddenly dark sky. "Looks like someone really got it wrong this time."

Predicting the weather in New England was always an iffy thing, especially when it came to bad weather. Leah just hoped the meteorologist had it right about this weekend. Her parents were throwing their annual Fourth of July bash. If weather similar to tonight's rolled in on Saturday, everything would have to be moved inside, and Mom hated when her plans changed at the last minute—a trait they both shared.

"Ms. Sherbrooke, Mr. Kincaid, it is so nice to see you both again this evening," the hostess greeted when they approached.

Regardless of the individual manning the hostess desk, he or she always recognized club members and addressed them by name. Considering the size of the country club, Leah found it rather remarkable.

"Would you prefer a table by a window or upstairs this evening?" the hostess asked.

"Either is fine," she replied.

The hostess led them through the dining room to a small table tucked away near a back corner. It was a table perfectly positioned for a romantic dinner for two, and Leah suspected the hostess assumed they were a couple rather than friends sharing a meal, especially since tonight wasn't the first time she'd seen them in here together.

Okay, perhaps that wasn't completely true. They weren't just friends, but good friends. Something she still found not so much odd but unique. Except for her two older brothers and numerous male cousins, she'd never had a close, platonic relationship with a guy. That wasn't to say she didn't have friends of the opposite sex, but those friends always remained more superficial. Her friendship with Gavin was far from that.

She hadn't expected to see or hear from Gavin again after she walked out of Harry and Gavin's condo. But the following afternoon, he called to ask how she was doing, and they'd ended up talking for almost an hour. Three days after their phone chat, she'd been restless. Rather than meet up with friends and again be on the receiving end of their looks of pity, she'd called Gavin and invited him to lunch. To this day she still couldn't say why she'd called him instead of visiting her cousin Callie, who only lived a few miles away and was usually too busy chasing after her young son to offer up looks of pity. Whatever the reason, she didn't regret her decision. Since then they'd engaged in countless conversations both in person and on the phone, gone for dinner numerous times, and played several rounds of golf at the country club they both belonged to.

"How was Gray's wedding last weekend?" Gavin inquired once they were both seated and the hostess was gone.

"Beautiful, and thankfully the weather cooperated."

The entire family had held its breath in the days leading up to her cousin Gray's and Kiera's wedding as meteorologists tracked a storm moving up over the Atlantic from the Caribbean. Thankfully, it had stalled somewhere off the coast of North Carolina, allowing the wedding to be held on the lawns of Cliff House in Newport as planned. The following day, though, the skies had opened up and dumped plenty of rain on southern New England before moving back out over the ocean.

"Brett even made it," she added, referring to her eldest brother. "I really didn't think he would. He missed both Trent's and Derek's weddings last year." As an officer in the United States Army, unfortunately Brett usually missed most family events. "And Curt and his girlfriend left before the ceremony even started. She had some kind of emergency at home. I have no idea what it was. Curt didn't share any details, and we haven't talked since."

Across the table, Gavin opened the menu the hostess had left him. "Is he still living up in New Hampshire or did you finally convince him to move back to Boston?"

"Still up there, and since his girlfriend lives next door, I don't see him moving anytime soon. He put his apartment in Boston on the market."

She'd tried talking some sense into Curt, but he'd refused to budge. Instead he invited her up to visit his latest project and the quaint—his word, not hers—town of Pelham, New Hampshire—something she had every intention of doing soon. Since they'd left so suddenly, she hadn't had much of a chance to get to know her older brother's new girlfriend and she wanted to rectify that. However, from the little she'd spoken with Taylor, she'd gotten the impression the woman was unlike any of Curt's past girlfriends. And since he'd brought her to not only Gray's wedding but also to a family-only gathering at their cousin's home a few weeks earlier, he was serious about Taylor Walker in a way he'd never been serious about a woman before.

Leah opened her own menu, although she already had a decent idea of what she wanted for dinner. "What about you? How was your week?" She scanned the list of entrées, noting the changes the restaurant had made since her last visit a week and a half ago.

"Hot."

At the sound of the single word in his smoky voice, a fluttering sensation that had nothing to do with being hungry sprang up in her belly.

"You were in Mississippi, right?" She set her menu aside so she could look at him, only to discover his dark, almost magnetic eyes focused solely on her and not his menu.

Gavin nodded, his gaze never leaving her face. "Jackson. Honestly, I don't know how people live down there in the summer. It gets hot and humid around here, but nothing compared to down there."

Their waitress appeared to take their dinner order, putting a temporary hold on their conversation. While he seemed oblivious to the fact, it didn't escape Leah that the woman was eyeing Gavin much the way a tigress eyed her prey just before she pounced.

An emotion bordering on jealousy slithered its way through her thoughts, and Leah cleared her throat. "I've changed my mind," she said once Gavin finished giving the woman his dinner selection, forcing her to look her way.

The tigress masquerading as a waitress turned her attention to Leah, but judging by her expression, she wasn't at all happy about it.

"Instead of the gorgonzola crusted filet, I'll have the seared tuna with gingered rice, please."

"Certainly," the waitress said with a slight nod as she took a step back. "And I'll bring out your appetizer as soon as it is ready."

"Almost went with the tuna myself," Gavin commented once they were alone. "But the porterhouse sounded too good today."

With the waitress no longer devouring Gavin with her eyes, the unpleasant emotion invading Leah's thoughts faded away. Maybe later she'd examine whatever she'd just experienced, because it wasn't the first time it had happened, but with him sitting across the table watching her, doing so now was impossible.

"What about this weekend? Any big plans?" Leah inquired.

He reached for his water glass and shook his head. "Catching up at the office."

"You are not." Any other weekend she'd accept his response, but not this one. "Saturday is the Fourth of July, Gavin. You know, cookouts and fireworks. Spending time with friends and family. Having fun."

"I know." He shrugged matter-of-factly before sipping his water. "And since the Fourth falls on a Saturday, the office will be empty until Tuesday morning. I can work and not be interrupted."

Leah admired how dedicated he was to Culloden, but seriously, the restaurant giant wouldn't go under if he took a few days off. "You can't work on the Fourth of July. Monday, sure, okay, if you insist, but not Saturday."

"I've got no other plans, and thanks to my business trip to Jackson, I'm behind on a few projects."

It was time for a little friendly intervention. He might be the chief development officer for the Culloden Company, but even he needed some downtime. "Well, you have plans now, my friend. Saturday, Mom is hosting her annual Fourth of July party in Newport. You're coming with me. It'll be fun."

MENTALLY GAVIN PUMPED his fist in the air. For the past three months he'd been fostering his friendship with Leah, waiting for the perfect opportunity to make his move. Considering the way things ended between her and Harry, he hadn't wanted to move too fast. Although it had been pure hell, he'd refrained from pursuing her the way he wanted, allowing her time to get past her breakup while at the same time getting to know him better. If she was inviting him along to her parents' house, perhaps the time had finally come to step things up.

"Shouldn't you check with her before you invite me?" His mom didn't hold many parties. When she did, the guest list was planned at least two months in advance, and she didn't take well to last-minute additions. He'd never met Judith Sherbrooke, but he wouldn't be surprised to learn she had that in common with Mom.

Leah waved a dismissive hand in his direction. "She's used to last-minute additions. And don't worry about this being a big family event. Mom invites a lot of her and Dad's friends too. You'll probably even know some."

Whether he knew anyone there or not didn't matter to him. The only person he cared about sat across from him.

She narrowed her eyes and pointed a finger at him. "And I'm warning you right now. If you say no or give me some other excuse, remember I know where you work and live. Don't think for a minute I won't storm your office and drag you to the party by your hair."

No need to drag me anywhere.

Gavin threw up both hands in defeat. "Just tell me the address and time and I'll be there. Promise."

"It's not that I don't trust you, but when it comes to taking a day off, I don't trust you, Gavin." There was no missing the trace of humor in her voice. "Meet me at my house Saturday morning around nine o'clock, and we'll drive to Newport together. We can spend the night at my parents' house and come back Sunday afternoon. They have plenty of room."

Showing up at her family's party unexpectedly was one thing, but staying the night was another matter. He'd happily make the three-plus hour drive back and forth with Leah, but he'd book himself a hotel room for the night.

"I'll meet you at your house, but I'll get a room nearby for Saturday night." There was no shortage of hotels in and around Newport.

Their waitress appeared with the prosciutto-wrapped mozzarella they'd ordered. Despite the fact Leah sat across from him, the waitress sized him up as if he was a prime piece of horseflesh she wanted to add to her stable.

"Is there anything else I can bring you at the moment?" the waitress asked, her eyes never leaving him.

"I'm fine, thank you. Leah?" When he transferred his gaze back across the table, the last thing he expected to see was an annoyed expression on Leah's face. Yet, with her jaw clenched tight and her lips forming a partial frown, it was the only word that came close to describing the look she wore.

Interesting. He'd given up trying to guess what went on in a woman's head a long time ago, but right now he'd love to know what was going through Leah's mind.

She gave the waitress a curt nod. "I'm fine too."

"Fabulous. I'll bring out your entrées when they are ready." The waitress sent him one last *I'm yours if you want me* look before walking away.

"Do you want to drive on Saturday or do you want me to?" he asked.

Leah's gaze trailed after the waitress briefly before her eyes turned back in his direction. "We can figure it out then." She added some of the appetizer to her plate and then pushed the rest closer to him. "I had this the last time I came. It's delicious."

GAVIN MASSAGED the back of his neck and stood. He'd arrived home from the country club three hours ago and gone straight into his office. Since then he hadn't moved from his desk. The cramps in his neck and back were telling him it was time to call it a night, even if he hadn't gotten as much accomplished as he'd hoped.

Switching off the lights, he left the room and headed for his bedroom. Tomorrow morning he'd get up a couple hours earlier than normal and get some extra work in. When he told Leah he had some catching up to do, he hadn't lied. The projects in Mississippi had dominated all his time while he was down there, meaning everything else had gone on hold. Then he'd gone straight from Jackson to his apartment in Providence, where he'd spent the weekend before coming back to New York late Sunday night. While in Providence he hadn't touched his laptop or his briefcase.

Before his ex-girlfriend's move to Rhode Island two years

ago, he'd spent time with Erin every chance he got. Unfortunately, now he only got to see his nine-year-old daughter every other weekend during the school year, assuming he wasn't traveling for business. In the summer he got to spend a little more time with her, but even then it was limited due to work obligations and the fact they lived four hours apart—a fact he hated but couldn't do much about, since Culloden's headquarters were located in New York City and Amber's promotion had taken her to Providence. Given the current situation, Gavin refused to let anything, including work, stop him from enjoying time with his daughter whenever he got the opportunity. Especially during their most recent visit, because he wouldn't see Erin again until close to the end of July. This morning she'd flown down to Florida with Amber and Amber's boyfriend to visit her family as well as the theme parks for a few weeks.

Until tonight, the only plus side he'd seen about the situation was that when Erin returned north, she'd be spending almost two full weeks with him in New York. His conversation with Leah tonight had him wondering if there might be a second silver lining to Erin being on vacation with her mom for most of the month.

He'd sensed Leah viewed him as more than a casual buddy she could rely on for a round of golf and dinner. Her insistence tonight that he join her rather than work over the holiday weekend reinforced his gut belief. And usually his gut didn't let him down.

Since he wouldn't be traveling back and forth to Providence this month, he could dedicate his attention to Leah and hopefully move their relationship in the direction he wanted. With a little luck, it'd be in a good place before Erin came and stayed with him, because as of now Leah didn't know he had a daughter.

Gavin changed the alarm on his phone and then tossed his

shoes in the closet. Not for the first time over the past few months, his conscience chastised him for not telling Leah about Erin. She'd talked about her family countless times during their conversations, but he'd kept Erin's existence to himself for two reasons. One, his relationship with his daughter was the most important thing in his life, and he didn't share the information with many people, especially women. He'd experienced firsthand a woman using the existence of a child to achieve her goals. He was eight when Dad met Joy. In the beginning she had acted as though she'd be the perfect stepmother, especially to Vivian. However, once Joy had the ring on her finger, she cut him, Vivian, and Harry out of her life and tried to write them out of their father's life too. At the time, Vivian had taken it the hardest because she'd grown to care a great deal about the woman. And Vivian's relationship with their dad had never been the same again, even though he'd divorced Joy after a year. Under no circumstances did Gavin ever want to put Erin in a similar situation. And two, from the start he'd gone out of his way to not discuss his family at all because of Leah's previous involvement with his half brother. Although he knew she would never take Harry back, and the guy had certainly tried, he didn't want to remind her they were related and in turn think he treated women the same way Harry did. Another bonus to not talking about his family was that Gavin could avoid mentioning his dad, a man whose cheating reputation was well known and not someone he wanted her to think he emulated.

Yeah, he'd gone out with plenty of women in college, but unlike his half brother, he'd never screwed around behind a girlfriend's back. He left that kind of behavior to Harry and their dad before his most recent marriage. At least, he believed Dad was faithful to Kerry, his fourth wife. When it came to Donald Kincaid and women, one could never be 100 percent certain. And honestly, he didn't want to know what his dad did or didn't do unless it involved the company.

So while Harry went out with half the female population in New York between the ages of twenty-five and thirty-five, Gavin's romantic life slowly deteriorated as his role in the family company grew. His relationship with Amber Wright had been the last committed one he had. It had ended more than eight years ago, not long after their daughter was born.

The more he got to know Leah, the more he wanted to see if he could change the relationship abyss his life had fallen into. And after biding his time for three months, he intended to plunge forward this weekend. Fingers crossed it wasn't too soon.

He switched off the lights and climbed into bed, once again grateful for the silence—something he'd missed during the months Harry lived with him. The guy thought nothing of blasting the television at one o'clock in the morning or having a guest arrive regardless of the time. They'd had more than one heated argument about both during his stay.

Rather than close his eyes, he stared into the darkness as the memory of Leah's face at dinner surfaced. No question about it, she'd been annoyed when the waitress delivered their appetizer and when she brought over their entrées. As far as he could tell, her annoyance hadn't popped up at any other time, suggesting there was a correlation between it and the waitress. Had the clear invitations she'd been sending his way been the cause of Leah's annoyance? Perhaps jealousy on Leah's part?

Hell, he'd experienced the green-eyed monster more than once when they'd been together and a guy hit on her. At least in Leah's case, she had nothing to be jealous about. She had his undivided attention.

Gavin pushed the memory aside and started on a mental list of everything he needed to accomplish between tomorrow and Saturday morning. He was almost done when the sound of an old-fashioned phone ringing interrupted him. Only a handful of people called him this late, including his twin sister, Vivian.

A quick look at the cell phone's screen confirmed the call was from her.

"First tell me you're somewhere besides the office," Vivian said after he answered the phone.

"Don't worry, Viv, I'm home." On occasion his twin sister was worse than their mom when it came to nagging him about how much time he spent at the office.

"Doing something besides work, I hope."

Reaching over, he switched on the bedside lamp and moved into a sitting position. "Trying to get some sleep, Mother." Whenever she started on him, he called her mother in an attempt to annoy her. It never failed.

"Yeah, I guess it is a little late out there," she admitted, suggesting she'd again failed to take into account the three-hour time difference between New York and California before she called him. "Sorry if I woke you."

"You didn't. So what's up?"

"Tomorrow I'm headed to Nantucket for the holiday weekend. Come and stay with me. We haven't spent time together in months."

Unlike him and Harry, Vivian had rejected a position at Culloden after college, opting to make her own way in the world. For the past few years, she'd been living and working in California. Despite their regular phone conversations, they hadn't spent any time together since St. Patrick's Day. He'd been in San Francisco in March for business and he'd stayed with her instead of at a hotel. If he didn't already have plans, he'd take her up on the offer and say to hell with work.

"Sorry, I can't. I've got plans for the Fourth."

"With who?" she asked, sounding suspicious. "Isn't Erin in Florida with her mom?"

Vivian made it sound like he didn't spend time with anyone except his daughter. While he didn't go out much, he was hardly a recluse.

"Is Harry throwing a party?" she inquired. Considering how often Harry liked to throw parties, it was a logical question.

"Yes, Erin is in Florida with Amber, and as far as I know Harry isn't throwing a party. But if he is, he didn't invite me." Even if he had, Gavin wouldn't attend. Harry's idea of a fun party and his were worlds apart.

"Spending the day in your office doesn't constitute plans, baby brother." All of ten minutes separated them, but Vivian still loved to tease him that technically he was younger than her. "Meet me on Nantucket. It'll be fun. Willow and her husband will be there. Brandy is coming too. And Parker and his fiancée are going to try to make it."

Willow and her younger sister Brandy had been friends with Vivian since college. He'd spent more than one weekend with them at his sister's house on Nantucket. Before Willow met and married Levi Jennings, Vivian had hoped something would develop between them. Although he liked Willow, he'd never been attracted to her. Since Willow's wedding last fall, Vivian had set her hopes on him and Brandy hitting it off. He didn't understand why Vivian was so dead-set on setting him up with her friends, but much like with Willow, he liked Brandy, but she wasn't his type.

"My day doesn't include work or the office," Gavin assured her. "Leah invited me to a party at her parents' house, so I'm heading to Newport. But thanks for the invite."

"Imaginary friends don't count," she tossed back jokingly.

"You're hilarious. Have you ever considered doing a stand-up comedy act?"

"Can you blame me for doubting you?" Vivian asked. "Not once during any of our recent conversations have you mentioned a girlfriend, and now suddenly you're going to a party at her parents' house."

You got me there.

He hadn't said anything about the friendship developing between him and Leah. Actually, he hadn't even mentioned her name during their conversations. Instead he'd focused on what was going on in Vivian's life and what his daughter was up to, because although his sister lived across the country, she adored her niece.

"Do I know this mystery woman?" Vivian didn't like to be left in the dark no matter the subject matter, but especially when it came to his romantic life.

"Yeah, you met Leah the night you stopped by." Back in February his sister had been in the city to see a show and popped in for a couple hours. Both Harry and Leah had been at the condo.

"Leah as in Leah Sherbrooke? Harry's girlfriend?"

Harry and Vivian had never been close, and it wasn't unusual for them to go several months without speaking. He'd assumed she'd seen or heard that their brother was now involved with runway supermodel Milan Novak. Well, at least he had been as of last week. Keeping up with Harry's love life required more effort than Gavin cared to exert.

"She dumped him about three months ago after she caught him with one of my neighbors. I think Harry's dating a model now," he explained.

Vivian snorted. "Big shocker there. Someday I hope he gets a taste of his own medicine." His twin had always been vocal in her opinion of how Harry treated the women he dated. "When did you two get together?"

"We're friends, Viv. We go golfing together and occasionally share a meal."

"I have a lot of friends, both male and female. Except for Willow and Brandy, I wouldn't invite any of them to a party at Mom's house unless there was something between us."

Gavin noticed she didn't mention parties at their dad's house. For as long as he could remember, Vivian and Dad had butted heads. Now unless the event Dad and Kerry were throwing was for Piper, their much-younger half sister, Vivian rarely attended anything at their father's house. That often included Thanksgiving and Christmas gatherings.

"And if you agreed to go, Gavin, she's more than another golfing buddy to you," she continued.

Vivian knew he wasn't one for big parties. Even in high school and college he'd preferred to hang around with a handful of close friends rather than a packed house full of people he didn't know.

"I'm taking it slow with her," Gavin admitted. There wasn't a person out there he trusted more than Vivian. Anything he said to her wouldn't go any farther. "Considering how things ended between her and Harry, it seemed like a good idea."

"Probably not a bad plan," she agreed. "How does she feel about you having a daughter?"

On the two occasions Gavin had shared that he was a father, both women had told him they weren't interested in sharing him with Erin. He couldn't see Leah saying anything remotely close to that. She seemed to value family. Actually, the whole Sherbrooke family was rumored to be extremely close despite its size.

"I haven't told her about Erin yet."

A tsking sound came through the phone. "Before things get serious, I recommend telling her. I don't know about Leah, but I'd hate to have a guy drop news like that on me after we've been together a few months. It would make me wonder what other secrets he's keeping."

He planned to not only tell her but also hopefully introduce her to Erin when the time was right. "Don't worry. I'll tell her soon."

"Well, have fun. And if your plans change, my door is open. No need to call. Just drop by."

Unless Leah called telling him she changed her mind, he wouldn't let anything keep him from spending the holiday weekend with her.

TWO

Leah dropped her overnight bag by the front door and headed for the kitchen. She'd called Gavin the night before and reminded him that if he didn't show up at her house by nine this morning, she'd drive into the city and get him. She half expected him to insist he had too much work and just couldn't take the weekend off. When he did, she had an argument all prepared.

He surprised her though. Instead of backing out, he laughed and promised to be there on time—not that he'd ever been anything but on time when they got together, unlike her ex-boyfriend. Even if it meant the difference between life and death, Harry would be late.

Before hanging up, she'd extended her mom's invitation for Gavin to stay at the house rather than in a hotel. As she'd expected, Mom had been more than happy to add one more person to the guest list. In Mom's opinion, when it came to a gathering like this, the more the merrier. Since so many of the people attending the party lived within driving distance, very few were spending the night. Despite the invite, Gavin again insisted he'd rather stay at a hotel. For reasons she couldn't fully label, she'd been disappointed. Rather than dwell on it though, she focused on the fact he was coming and she'd be able to enjoy his company—something she found herself wanting to do more and more lately.

She managed to finish half her iced tea, her favorite summer morning drink, before the console on the kitchen wall beeped, alerting her to someone at the door. She ignored the little jig her stomach suddenly started doing and headed down the hallway.

"Right on time," she greeted. "Come on in."

Gavin dropped his cell phone into a pocket and slipped his sunglasses onto his head as he stepped inside. "I would've been here earlier, but I got an unexpected visit from my dad. I finally had to kick him out."

"No worries. I overslept this morning and only finished packing about ten minutes ago. I haven't even eaten breakfast yet. I thought we could grab something on the way."

She almost never overslept, but the night before what was supposed to be a quick visit with Callie and her family had turned into the opposite. Despite her plans to get home early and pack, she hadn't walked through the door until well after two this morning.

"Thanks to Dad, I never got around to it either, so I was going to suggest we stop at Café Sorell before we get on the road," Gavin admitted. "Unless you prefer somewhere else."

"No, they have great pastries." She tried to keep her eyes on his face, but this morning she was finding it quite the challenge. The man really belonged in some magazine advertising underwear instead of behind a desk.

"Are you ready to go or do you need a few more minutes?" he asked, oblivious to her struggles.

"Good to go. Do you want to drive or should I?"

Most days she didn't mind being behind the wheel for a long drive. This morning she'd much rather be in the passenger seat so she could keep her eyes focused on him instead of the road, but since she'd invited him along, it only seemed fair she offer to tackle the three-and-a-half-hour drive to Newport.

Taking a step back toward the door, he shrugged. "You look tired. I don't mind doing it." He picked up the overnight bag she'd left on the floor. "Is this it?"

She nodded. "I'll meet you outside. I need to grab my purse."

Through the windshield she saw the cell phone glued to Gavin's ear as she approached his car. Although the call could be a friendly one, she put her money on it having something to do with work. Perhaps this weekend she'd find a way for the device to go missing until it was time to head home. Really, any projects he had going on could take a vacation for two days.

Whatever the call was about, he ended it as she opened the door.

"Please tell me you weren't discussing business." Leah climbed into the air-conditioned vehicle, the leather cool against her bare legs.

"No, just talking to a friend. They wanted to share some news with me." He started the engine and drove down the long driveway.

It didn't go unnoticed that Gavin didn't mention the friend's name or give any hint whether it was a male or female friend. "Good news, I hope," she inquired, her curiosity getting the better of her this morning.

"Uh, yeah I guess." Gavin turned left out of the driveway and proceeded down the street. "She got engaged last night."

"Engagements are usually good news." Despite all the time she'd spent with Gavin, he'd only mentioned a handful of friends, and they'd all been male. "She must be a close friend if she called this morning to tell you."

Rather than immediately answer, he adjusted the air vent near the steering wheel. "I've known Amber a long time."

Knowing someone for years didn't mean you had a close relationship with her. And although absolutely none of her business, she wanted to know just how close he and Amber were. "Does she live near you?"

"Not anymore. She moved to Rhode Island about two years ago. She lives in Providence."

A burst of relief washed over her. If he had to have a close female friend, engaged or not, Leah preferred she wasn't living right next door to him.

You have no claim on him, she reminded herself. They were friends, nothing more. Whatever did or didn't exist between him and other women didn't affect her. Before she said something she'd later regret, she'd better change the subject.

"Does your dad make surprise visits like he did today a lot?" Despite dating Harry for two and a half months, she'd only met Donald Kincaid once and it'd been a chance encounter at a restaurant.

"Occasionally. He did it more when Harry was living with me. Dad's always been closer to him than me."

She was 99 percent certain this was the first time since the afternoon she caught Harry with another woman that Gavin had mentioned his half brother. Come to think of it, he didn't talk about his family much. Leah couldn't help but wonder if her and Harry's previous relationship was the reason behind it.

"You've got the condo to yourself again?" She'd assumed Harry had left Gavin's and moved into his new house by now. It'd been more than half completed when they broke up. But when it came to construction, setbacks happened all the time. When she'd had her own house remodeled, it took a month longer then planned.

Gavin pulled into the parking lot of the nearby café. "Yes, thank God. Harry moved out the beginning of June. And if he hadn't, I might have checked into a hotel until he did." He turned off the engine and looked at her. "If he ever asks to stay with me again, I'll barricade the door."

Whenever she'd been there, it had appeared as though they'd been coexisting peacefully despite their polar opposite personalities. Gavin's comments told a different story. "It's not always easy living with someone."

"Vivian, I could handle living with," Gavin said as he reached for his door handle. "We're a lot alike. I think the only thing Harry and I have in common is that we have the same father."

From what she'd seen, Leah agreed with Gavin's assessment of him and his half brother. "I've only met Vivian once. Who is older, you or her?"

He opened the café door and held it for her. "She is," he answered, following her inside. "By ten minutes, and she never lets me forget it."

Leah chuckled. "Must be a twin thing. Derek loves to remind Allison he's older too. It drives her crazy," she explained, referring to her cousins. "Too bad Allison won't be there today. The two of you could commiserate with each other."

She stopped in front of the display case. Everything from croissants and muffins to cinnamon rolls and breakfast sandwiches was on display.

"Maybe some other time," he replied.

His comment had her looking away from the tasty treats and toward him. "You probably usually work on New Year's Eve, but not this year, my friend. It might be months away, but I'm inviting you now to the New Year's Eve party at Cliff House. Don't worry, I'll remind you a lot between now and then so you won't forget. Allison will be there. She never misses it. The two of you can complain about how difficult it is to be the younger twin then."

New Year's Eve was a little more than five months away. A lot could happen in five months. Regardless, she expected Gavin to still be a part of her life, and she wanted him to ring in the New Year with her.

"I'll put it on my calendar." He turned toward the food on display. "Any ideas for breakfast?"

She'd stopped in Café Sorell before and to date she'd never been disappointed with anything she picked. "I'm going with the cinnamon roll and a double espresso," she answered, not bothering to look away from him.

He always looked handsome, but this morning there was something different about him. She couldn't put her finger on it, but since he walked though her front door, she'd been having trouble keeping her eyes off him—a fact she hoped he didn't notice, because if he did it was going to be a long, awkward weekend.

He approached the counter and smiled at the young woman behind it. On cue she smiled back, and it was impossible to miss the light pink hue spreading across her cheeks. "We'll have two cinnamon rolls and two double espressos to go, please," he said.

With a nod the employee walked away. As she prepared their order, she threw countless looks Gavin's way—looks he couldn't have missed if Leah noticed them. Much like the night at the country club restaurant, she found herself grinding her teeth. If she kept reacting this way every time a member of the opposite sex looked his way this weekend, she was going to be in desperate need of a dentist Monday morning.

UNLIKE CLIFF HOUSE, which had been built by one of Leah's ancestors in 1895 to resemble Alexander Palace in Russia and was currently owned by her Uncle Warren, her parents' home in Newport didn't look as if it belonged in a history book. After purchasing the property on Ocean Drive twenty years ago following a fire that destroyed most of the original structure, they'd torn down what was left and started over. It took them a couple years to design and build exactly what they wanted, but now a gorgeous 14,000 square foot home sat overlooking the Atlantic Ocean. Despite the size, it felt like a true home instead of museum, which was how Cliff House always felt to her.

"It's your next right," Leah said as they drove down the street.

In anticipation of guests, the front gates had been left open, and Gavin drove up the horseshoe-shaped driveway. Several of the guests had already arrived judging by the number of cars parked, and Leah surveyed the collection. Many she recognized as belonging to family members, but a few definitely belonged to her parents' friends and neighbors.

Gavin parked next to a SUV with New Hampshire plates. Although she'd never seen the vehicle before, she guessed it belonged to Curt. After all, who else did her parents know in New Hampshire?

"I think my brother and his girlfriend are here." She pointed to the vehicle. "Have you ever met Curt?" She'd never introduced him to any of her family, but that didn't mean he'd never met them elsewhere.

"Once, about a year ago. I escorted my mom to a Helping Hands fundraiser in Providence because Clark was away on business. Your brother was there."

She'd never met his mom, Faith Williamson, or her second husband, Clark, but she knew they lived in Rhode Island and were supporters of Helping Hands, a foundation started by her great-grandmother and currently run by her Aunt Marilyn.

Mom and Dad would do everything to make Gavin feel comfortable this weekend, but she was glad he'd at least met one family member before today.

"Do you think this is everyone?" He nodded toward the many cars parked around them as they walked toward the front steps.

Leah quickly surveyed the collection again. "Doubt it."

"When you said Fourth of July bash, you meant it."

She didn't bother ringing the bell. Instead she opened the door and stepped inside the cool air-conditioned home. "Mom goes all out every year for this party. The ones she throws at the holidays are much smaller."

IF EVERYTHING WENT the way Gavin hoped, he'd find out for himself in a few months.

He followed her across the two-story open foyer. Although a stunning home, it wasn't ostentatious, which was the only word to adequately describe his father's home since his wife had redecorated. Considering the few pictures he'd seen of Cliff House, her uncle's home, he'd expected her parents' house to be decked out with marble columns and gilded ceilings. As far as he could see, neither existed here.

Leah paused at the bottom of one curved staircase. "I'm just going to run this up to my room. I'll be right back. Feel free to wait here or head outside. Whatever you're more comfortable with."

He'd never met Judith Sherbrooke, but he recognized Leah's mom right away. Although Judith had dark brown hair and dark eyes and stood at least four or five inches taller than Leah, the shape of their faces and eyes were the same.

"Good, you're here, Leah," she greeted.

At the sound of her mom's voice, Leah left her overnight bag on the floor and moved away from the stairs and back toward him.

Judith approached him and smiled, causing her to resemble Leah even more.

"You must be Gavin." Judith extended her hand toward him. "I'm Judith, Leah's mother. I'm glad you were able to join us today."

"Thank you for having me. It's been a long time since I went to a Fourth of July party," he said.

After hugging her mom, Leah stepped closer and nudged him in the side. "Or any party for that matter. I told him if he didn't come today, I'd drag him out of the office."

That's what you think. "Guilty as charged," he replied.

"Sounds like someone else we know and love," Judith commented affectionately. "No matter. You're here now. Are you sure you don't want to spend the night? We have the room, Gavin."

Yeah, on this one, no one, not even Leah, was going to get him to budge. "I appreciate the offer, but I already reserved a room at a hotel."

"Well, if you change your mind the offer stands," Judith commented before turning her gaze toward Leah. "If you want to bring your bag upstairs, I'll bring Gavin outside and start introducing him to everyone."

Like the perfect hostess, Judith kept up a steady conversation as she led him through the house and outside. Although he'd never met many of the people already gathered, thanks to the media he recognized most of them, including several of Leah's cousins and her father, who was speaking with an older gentleman he didn't recognize.

With her husband occupied, Judith led him over to Leah's older brother. Although he was standing alone, Curt's attention was focused on someone on the beach. "Curt, I'd like you to meet Gavin. He's a friend of Leah's."

Sherbrooke blue eyes identical to Leah's swung his way, and he held Gavin's gaze for a moment before extending his hand. "Nice to see you again."

"Excellent, you already know each other," Judith said before she frowned, her eyes focused on something or someone across the deck. "Do you mind introducing him to everyone? Janet is waving me over. She must need something."

Gavin spotted a woman approximately his mom's age waving at Judith. Judging by Judith's tone, it wasn't the first time Janet needed something today.

"Sure," Curt answered. It was a simple one-word answer, yet something in his voice told Gavin to be on guard.

Curt waited until his mom left before speaking again. "When I invited Leah to stay at my place this weekend, she never mentioned bringing a date to the party."

He didn't know if she'd intentionally left out the information or if she invited him after talking to Curt. "My coming along today was a last-minute thing," Gavin explained.

"Last-minute? My sister?" He sounded shocked. "Leah usually plans everything out in advance."

Gavin agreed. At least in the months he'd known her, Leah had never seemed to do anything spontaneous. "When she found out on Tuesday that I planned on working today, she invited me."

"We spoke on Thursday." Curt's expression gave no hint at what he was thinking. "Are you staying the whole weekend?"

"Just tonight. We plan on driving back in the morning."

Leah's brother shoved his hands in his front pockets. "Think about staying another night. The two of you can stop by and visit with Taylor, Reese, and me. We're here until Wednesday."

He knew Taylor was Curt's girlfriend, but he had no idea who Reese was. "Whatever your sister wants." He'd planned to finish up the work leftover from last week when he got back to the city on Sunday, but if Leah wanted to stick around longer, he wouldn't argue. It would give him more time with her.

"I'll talk to her when I see her. C'mon, I'll introduce you to Taylor. She's helping the kids build sandcastles."

Gavin saw several children of various ages on the beach, along with a handful of adults. He assumed some of the children were Leah's relatives, but he didn't think they all were. There seemed to be too many.

"Are you still living in New York?" Curt asked as they made their way across the grass and past other guests.

He nodded. "Yeah, when I'm not traveling."

Curt laughed. "Best part about not being in the corporate world anymore."

"Leah mentioned you left Nichols Investment back in the spring."

"One of the best decisions I ever made." He stopped when they reached the edge of the grass. "Harry still living with you?"

If Curt knew Harry had been living with him, he'd gotten the information from Leah. Had Leah also told her brother why she'd broken up with the guy? If family was as important to Leah as it seemed, he didn't want her brother or anyone else disliking him because of how his half brother had treated her.

"He moved out last month," Gavin answered. "And he won't be coming back."

"Too alike to live together?"

"Just the opposite."

Curt waved back at a young girl on the beach. "We better get going, or Reese will come and get me."

The girl waving looked about the same age as his daughter. "Most children are not known for their patience," Gavin commented, following Curt across the sand.

"Sounds like you're speaking from experience."

"I have a half sister who will be eleven in August. When she was younger, she couldn't wait for anything or anybody." He wasn't lying; Piper was almost eleven. However, when he'd made the comment he'd been thinking of Erin, not his half sister. "She's not much better now."

Curt introduced him first to Taylor, who was seated on the ground next to a well-thought-out sandcastle. It had a large square structure in the center with several pathways leading to various other buildings. A wall surrounded much of it. Seashells, tiny pebbles, and various bird feathers had been used to decorate the project.

Before Curt got around to introducing Gavin to anyone else, Leah joined them. "Sorry, I got cornered by Mrs. Clark on my way outside." She sounded a little out of breath. "Mom and she have been friends for a long time. I haven't seen her since last summer," she explained.

"Surprised you got away. Did she show you all the pictures of her grandchildren?" Curt asked. "She got me not long after we arrived. I saw at least fifty pictures before Mom rescued me."

"He's exaggerating." Taylor stood and put an arm around Curt's waist. "She didn't show you anywhere close to that many."

"With Mrs. Clark, you never know." Leah stepped closer to the sandcastle and knelt down to get a better look. "Fabulous castle. Did you build it?" she asked the girl Gavin assumed was Reese.

"Auntie Taylor's helping me," the girl answered.

Curt crouched down next to the young girl. "Leah, this is Reese, Taylor's niece." He ruffled the girl's hair, giving Gavin the impression Curt spent a decent amount of time around the child even though she was only his girlfriend's niece. "Short stuff, this is my sister."

Reese smiled, revealing the large gap where her two front teeth used to be. "Hi. Do you want to help me finish?"

Leah reached for one of the buckets. "I'd love to. Gavin, do you want to help us?"

It looked finished to him, but what did he know. "Building castles is one of my specialties." He dropped to the ground next to Leah and grabbed a plastic shovel. "What else needs to be done?"

Reese didn't hesitate to give him and Leah instructions, reminding him considerably of his daughter. Whenever possible Erin loved to be in charge. By the way Reese was giving out orders, it appeared she did too. Come to think of it, Piper did as well, so maybe it was a trait all girls around their age shared.

"Looks like we've got a lot of work to do, Gavin." Leah caught his eye and smiled. "We better get to it." She started to fill her bucket with sand. "Curt, are you going to help or just sit there and watch?"

He put his arm around Reese's shoulders and winked at her. "Reese and I are going to supervise, right, short stuff?"

She nodded. "Right."

Leah rolled her eyes and continued to fill the bucket. "Some things never change."

Despite Reese's agreement that she'd supervise while Taylor, Gavin, and Leah did the heavy lifting, she joined in after only a few minutes. Not long after, Curt got down to work as well. With everyone's attention either on constructing more buildings or making the bridge that would connect the two segments, Leah moved closer to Gavin.

"Sorry I left you alone with him for so long," she whispered in his ear.

Under different circumstances it would've been the perfect opportunity to kiss her. Unfortunately, they had a full audience.

"Don't worry about it. Your brother invited us to his place tomorrow." Since she'd whispered, Gavin assumed Leah didn't want Curt to hear their conversation, so he kept his voice low too.

Leah shot a look in her brother's direction, then moved another inch or two closer, and he caught the barest hint of either her shampoo or perfume. "Curt actually invited me to stay with him and Taylor this weekend. I considered it, but figured they might want their privacy. I didn't know Reese was going to be there too."

"If you want to head over tomorrow, it's fine with me. We can drive back on Monday morning," he offered.

She reached out and placed her hand on his forehead. The innocent touch set his skin on fire. "You don't feel warm. Are you feeling okay? Have you spent too much time in the sun? Maybe you should go sit in the shade and have some cold water. Or maybe you should go for a quick swim."

He might not feel warm on the outside, but internally he was burning up. "We're here. We might as well have fun."

Leah shifted back and gave him a quick visual once-over. "Who are you and what have you done with the real Gavin Kincaid?" she asked with suspicion.

"Locked him in the closet. I'm his smarter and handsomer twin."

She grinned, causing the dimple in her right cheek to appear. "If that's the case, I'll tell Curt we'll be over tomorrow before your double gets free and spoils all our fun."

THREE

When she'd come outside earlier and spotted Gavin and Curt talking, she'd cursed her rotten luck. She liked her mom's friend, Lucy Clark, but the woman loved to talk about her grandchildren. Most of the time, Leah didn't mind hearing about them or seeing the proud grandmother's latest pictures. Today had been a different story.

Although Curt didn't take the protective big brother role quite as far as her cousins did, he'd been known to interrogate her dates, and since she'd brought him along today, Curt and probably everyone else here would assume there was more between her and Gavin than mere friendship.

Rather than risk having a family member ask Gavin anything about their relationship and make him uncomfortable, she'd stayed next to him ever since joining him on the beach over two hours ago. But in desperate need of a bathroom break, she left him talking to Courtney and Juliette. Of all of her cousins there, Leah trusted them the most to behave themselves while she was gone.

"Hey, I've been looking for you."

Curt's statement brought her to a standstill when she came

out of the bathroom. "You found me." *Unfortunately*, she mentally added.

She loved her brother, but at the moment she didn't want to stand around and have a long heart-to-heart. "I just needed a quick bathroom break."

She tried to walk past him before he started up a real conversation and kept her inside any longer than necessary. He grabbed her hand though, forcing her to stop.

"No need to rush. Gavin can take care of himself." Releasing her hand, he crossed his arms over his chest and leaned against the wall. He wore a serious expression, and she suspected he'd decided it was time to be the protective older brother.

"I wasn't rushing because of him. It's a beautiful day, and I want to enjoy it. Shouldn't you be outside doing the same with Taylor and Reese?"

Curt's left eyebrow inched up. The tiny gesture annoyed Leah to no end as usual. She couldn't say why it did, but it did.

"Are you sure it's a good idea to get involved with your ex-boyfriend's brother?"

Yep, he was putting on his big brother cap this afternoon. "Harry and Gavin are half brothers. They have different mothers." She intentionally avoided answering his question simply to annoy him. After all, annoying one's brother was in the little sister job description.

"Minor technicality and you know it, Leah. Harry proved he's just like his father. I'd say there's a good chance Gavin is too," Curt said before she could set him straight. "I don't want you to get hurt again."

Why did I ever tell him? Thanks to her big mouth, Curt knew that both Harry and Benedict, her boyfriend before Harry, had cheated on her.

"We're not together, so relax. Gavin and I are just good

friends." While she appreciated Curt's concern, she wanted him to know it wasn't necessary. "But even if we were, Gavin's the exact opposite of Harry in every way imaginable." She started walking and hoped he dropped the subject. "Come on, let's head back out."

Curt fell into step next to her. "Not buying it, sis."

Right now she didn't care if he believed her or not. She and Gavin knew the truth. She opened the door and stepped out onto the lower deck. The scent of whatever was on the grill immediately caught her attention and her stomach rumbled. She ate in some of the best restaurants on a regular basis, yet there was something about food cooked on a grill that got her every time.

"You've never brought a friend, male or female, to any of Mom's parties," he continued, obviously not ready to drop the matter. "Only guys you're involved with. Something is up between you two."

Ignoring Curt, Leah searched the gathering for Gavin and her cousins, because they weren't standing where she left them. Had they walked down to the water? With lunch being served, the beach would be less crowded.

She headed for the stairs then stopped abruptly. "Seriously!"

Of all the men present, Tasha Marshall had to be talking to Gavin. Leah had known Tasha, the daughter of close family friends, forever. Despite the closeness of the two families, she'd never considered Tasha a friend. Rather she thought of her as an immature annoyance that showed up at a lot of family functions with one thing in mind: catching an unmarried Sherbrooke male. It didn't really seem to matter which one either. For years she'd chased after Leah's cousin Jake. When he got married, she proceeded to go after Trent, followed by first Gray and then Derek. Actually, she'd even tried to buy Derek at a bachelor auction the Helping Hands

Foundation held as a fundraiser. With all three of them happily married now as well, Leah had assumed Tasha would turn her attention to either Curt or her cousin Alec, since Brett was rarely around. Judging by how close Tasha was standing to Gavin and the fact she kept touching his arm, she'd decided to branch out.

"What's wrong?" Curt asked, dropping the subject of her and Gavin's relationship for the moment.

"That," she hissed and gestured in the general direction of Tasha and Gavin.

He patted her affectionately on the shoulder. "I'll let you handle that one. I've managed to stay under her radar today, and I'd prefer to keep it that way."

"Chicken."

"Hey, if it keeps me from being her next prey, you better believe it. Have fun. I'll talk to you later."

Leah resisted the urge to stick her tongue out as she watched Curt walk away. They might both be adults, but sometimes her brother could still be as annoying as when they were children.

As she approached Gavin and Tasha, Leah considered the best way to extract him. Countless times in the past she'd thought it was a shame Gavin didn't have a special person in his life. Once or twice she even considered setting him up with either Courtney or Juliette. And since he wasn't trying to get away from Tasha, it was possible he wanted to get to know her better. If that was the case, she shouldn't interfere. Instead she should go and visit with some of the other party guests and let things between Gavin and Tasha develop.

Unfortunately, the idea of them together had her mentally screaming. Leah didn't know who the right woman for Gavin was, but she knew it certainly wasn't Tasha Marshall. Since Gavin didn't know Tasha, it was up to her to save him. After all, friends should look out for each other. If she found herself in a similar situation, she hoped Gavin would step in and help her out.

"Hey, Tasha," Leah greeted, stopping next to Gavin. She didn't pause to think before putting an arm around his waist. She felt Gavin's back stiffen, but he didn't pull away. "How have you been? I don't think I've seen you since my uncle's New Year's Eve party."

Tasha offered up a less than enthusiastic smile. "I'm well. I'm moving to Manhattan at the end of the summer. Until then I'm staying on Martha's Vineyard."

"Lucky you. I haven't been to the island in ages." Leah glanced in Gavin's direction. His expression didn't suggest he was annoyed by her sudden interruption. "We should try to get over there before it gets too cold. Sara will let us use her and Christopher's house for a weekend. They hardly ever visit the island."

Gavin didn't hesitate to nod. Perhaps catching on to Leah's plan, he put an arm around her, causing her heart to flutter wildly in her chest. "Sounds like an excellent idea. I've never been there."

What the heck? This was Gavin. Her friend. Nothing more, nothing less. Her heart shouldn't be doing a tap dance routine against her rib cage.

Leah cleared her throat and tried to think up an appropriate response. "Really? Never? You'll love it. I'll call Sara tomorrow and see when we can use the house."

They chatted for a few more minutes before Tasha left them alone, no doubt in search of a single Sherbrooke male. The moment they were alone, Gavin moved so they faced each other. Although they were no longer touching, her skin tingled where his arm had been.

"Friend of yours?" he asked, nodding in the direction Tasha had walked.

"More like a family friend. Her father is Senator Richard

Marshall. He went to school with my dad and uncles. I've known her forever, but we never spend time together except at parties like this." Leah's eyes locked with his. Before this moment, she'd never wished she could read someone's thoughts. Now she'd pay anything for the ability.

"Gotcha."

At the single-word response, Leah's eyes dropped to his lips, and she wondered how he'd react if she kissed him.

Before it registered what she was doing, Leah stepped closer. "She usually pours herself all over any single male named Sherbrooke, but I think you were her prey for today. A fact Curt is very happy about, by the way."

Gavin's hands slipped up her arms, bringing her closer and eliminating whatever space remained between them. "I'm glad you rescued me then." Gently, he brushed several loose strands of hair back behind her ears. "It's a little crowded up here. Do you want to go for a walk on the beach?"

"Love to." Was that really her voice? She sounded breathless.

He smiled, causing the simple tap routine her heart was doing to change to something that would make the world-famous Rockettes jealous. Without another word, he took her hand, sending a warm shiver up her arm and straight through her body.

Neither spoke as they made their way off the deck and down to the sand. With lunch being served, most of the guests had deserted the beach. Left off-balance by the emotions floating around in her body, Leah shot a few glances in Gavin's direction, hoping for some clue as to what was going on in his head.

Had he felt the pull between them on the deck or had she imagined it?

At the moment, all she could see was his profile, and it wasn't telling her anything. On the deck, though, his expression had suggested he wanted to kiss her. And although she shouldn't want him to kiss her because they were friends and friends didn't kiss, she couldn't think of much else.

"I spend so much time in an office, I sometimes forget how much I love the outdoors." He stopped not far from the sandcastle they helped Reese build earlier. Although the buckets and shovels were still near the structure, at least for the moment the girl was gone. Leah guessed she'd gone up to get lunch along with the other party guests. "If not for you, I'd be sitting inside an office right now. Thanks again for inviting me," he continued.

Gavin released her hand. The loss of physical contact was an unpleasant jolt to her system. Leah was about to reach for it again when he moved, blocking the view of everything but him. Face-to-face, he settled a large hand on either side of her waist, and an almost tangible energy buzzed between them.

He's got to feel it too. I can't be the only one.

She fought the urge to reach out and trace his lips with her finger and instead curled her hands into fists by her sides, perhaps the safest place for them at the moment. "I'm glad you came." Much like on the deck, she barely recognized her voice.

Slowly he lowered his face toward hers. "Trust me, there is no other place I want to be." He brushed his lips against hers. The kiss was gentle and undemanding, yet it sent her emotions into a whirlwind, and she reached for him.

KISSING LEAH with an audience in the background hadn't been his plan. Instead he'd hoped to get her alone, perhaps right before he left for his hotel tonight, but when she put her arm around him on the deck, every one of his well-thought-out ideas jumped out the window along with much of his self-control. Getting her at least somewhat alone took center stage in his mind. Since the beach was temporarily deserted, it seemed like the best spot.

Warm hands settled on his upper arms a moment before Leah stepped closer, her breasts touching his chest. Instantly visions of him peeling her T-shirt off so he could taste them, much the way he was tasting her lips, taunted him. Unable to do what he truly wanted, he locked his hands against her spine before they got any wild ideas of their own and went exploring.

Raising his mouth from Leah's, Gavin waited. Slowly Leah opened her eyes and met his gaze. The heat he saw glowing in them was a reflection of the desire burning inside him.

Tilting her head, she studied him for a moment. "I was thinking about setting you up with either my cousin Courtney or Juliette."

Evidently he needed to work harder at showing her how he felt if she wanted to discuss setting him up with another woman seconds after they kissed. With her in his arms, he couldn't think of a better time to do it.

"But I can't do it," she continued with a slight shake of her head.

"Good, because but I'm interested in someone else." Gavin started toward her lips. "I've been —"

Leah pressed her lips against his, cutting off the rest of his sentence. His first instinct was to take control and kick up the intensity of the kiss. Instead of doing what he wanted, he left the reins in Leah's hands.

She didn't disappointment.

Soon what started as a whisper of a kiss changed, and she traced his lips with her tongue, urging him to open for her. When he parted his lips, she dipped her tongue inside. Gavin groaned, the sound lost in her mouth. After months of waiting, he not only had Leah in his arms, but if her kiss was any indication, she wanted him as much he wanted her.

"Do you guys want to help us some more on the sandcastle?" a girl's voice asked.

The question was an unpleasant reminder that not only were they not alone, but there were children around. He groaned again, although this time it had nothing to do with the passion setting him on fire.

They pulled away at the same time to find Reese looking at them, an expectant expression on her face. Curt and Taylor were on their way toward them too. The expression on her brother's face was much less friendly than it had been earlier.

Reese didn't wait for an answer before dropping to her knees and reaching for a plastic bucket. "I want to build a south wing."

Leah leaned in. "I don't mind helping. Do you?" she whispered.

While he'd love to have some private time with her, Leah's willingness to help a little girl she barely knew build a sandcastle suggested she'd accept his daughter when the time came.

Shaking his head, Gavin picked up two buckets and handed one to Leah. "Reese, we're awaiting your instructions."

The bright smile Reese gave them instantly had him missing Erin and wishing she was here rather than in Florida with her mom.

"You guys can start on the center tower for the new wing." Reese looked over at Curt and Taylor as they joined them around the building site. "Gavin and Leah said they'll help us." She handed Curt a bright pink plastic shovel, which he accepted without hesitation. "Curt, you can start on the bridge connecting the south wing to the main one."

Curt saluted her with the shovel. "On it, short stuff."

Not for the first time today, Gavin wondered about the relationship between Taylor, her niece, and Curt. It was clear Leah's brother and the little girl were comfortable around each other, and if the guy had a special nickname for Reese, he must spend a considerable amount of time around her. Considering this was Taylor's niece and not her daughter, Gavin found it odd.

Reese gave Taylor one of the tiny square buckets on the sand. "Auntie Taylor, we'll work on the castle stables."

Reese chatted away as they worked, telling them all about everything, from her time at camp the week before to how much she was looking forward to the fireworks tonight. Each time she laughed or smiled, Gavin was again reminded of his daughter. They'd done a lot of things together, but they'd never built a sandcastle. He'd never even taken her to a beach. When she came to stay in August, he'd have to rectify that. Hopefully Leah would accompany them.

Gavin shoveled more sand into the bucket. With the center tower of the south wing complete, Reese wanted him and Leah to start on the towers that would stand in each of the four corners. So far they'd completed one.

"She has my brother wrapped around her little finger." Leah's leg brushed against his as she leaned in and whispered in his ear.

Some would say the same thing about his daughter. There wasn't anything Gavin wouldn't do for her. "Little girls have a way of doing that."

"Yeah, I can see you doing anything Piper asked you too," she replied.

For now he'd let her assume his comment stemmed from his relationship with his much younger half sister. Soon he'd tell her about his daughter. He'd almost done it this morning when Erin called to tell him Amber had gotten engaged. Instead, when Leah asked, he told her the call was from

Amber, because it hadn't seemed like the right time to tell her he was a father.

"What's a brother for, especially an older one?" he asked.

"Curt and Brett have always thought it was their job to drive me nuts."

He sensed eyes on them. Even before checking, he knew he'd find Leah's brother watching them. Sure enough, when he glanced up he found Curt staring at him, and he instantly recognized the pure brotherly concern etched on the other man's face. It was an emotion he'd felt numerous times on behalf of both Vivian and Piper. Holding Curt's gaze, he nodded before turning his attention back to Leah.

"They only do it because they care about you," Gavin explained.

"Oh, I know. And trust me, I've also made sure to fulfill my duties as an annoying little sister." The mischievous smile made him wonder just what types of things she'd done to Curt and Brett over the years.

"Something tells me you have some great stories to share." Before he could ask if she'd care to share, his phone rang. As much as he didn't want to interrupt the fun, he pulled the device out and checked the caller ID. Amber's name was on the screen, but he doubted the caller was actually his ex-girlfriend. More likely it was Erin calling him again. A call from his dad or mom he'd consider ignoring, but not one from his daughter. "Sorry, I need to take this. It's my dad." He hated to lie, but what other option did he have?

Leah nudged him in the side. "It better be him. If I find out later it's work, you're in big trouble."

He wanted to kiss her, but with Curt's gaze still locked on him, Gavin opted for a smile instead. Pressing the green talk icon, he stood. "Be right back."

Gavin walked back up toward the house and listened as Erin filled him in on all the rides she'd gone on so far today.

By the sound of it, she was having a blast on vacation. While things hadn't worked out between him and Amber, he couldn't deny that she was a fabulous mom to their daughter, and Todd treated Erin like a daughter. So although he selfishly didn't love the idea of Erin having a stepfather in her life, he was genuinely happy for his ex-girlfriend and her new fiancé.

"I can't wait to see the pictures," he said, darting to the left when he spotted Tasha Marshall. The last thing he wanted was to get corned by her again, although perhaps he owed her a thank-you for her unintended help earlier. It hadn't been until Leah saw him and Tasha talking that she'd given him a clear sign her feelings for him ran deeper than mere friendship.

FOUR

From the comfort of a beach chair, Leah watched Gavin jump and hit the volleyball back over the net toward her cousin Jake. They'd asked her to play too, but she'd played enough sports with her family to know that what started out as friendly games quickly became extremely competitive. Sometimes she was up for that, and other times she preferred to sit back and watch her various male relatives get all worked up. Today not only wasn't she up for a competitive volleyball match, but by sitting on the sidelines she was able to work on her tan, and more importantly study Gavin half naked—an activity she found most enjoyable.

"Does he live in Providence?" Courtney asked. She'd opted not to play volleyball as well and sat next to her.

Leah's eyes followed the ball over the net and toward her cousin Trent, who managed to save it before it hit the sand. "Who?"

"Your boyfriend, Gavin. And don't tell me he's not. I saw you rush in to save him from Tasha. I swear I only left him alone for a minute to get a drink and she swooped in. If I'd known she'd try something, I would've waited until you got back. I assumed she'd be on the prowl for either Curt or Alec today."

When Curt had cornered her and insisted something was up between her and Gavin, she denied it. She couldn't deny it now, not after the kiss they shared on the beach. "I think Taylor's presence saved Curt today. And Alec just got here, so I can't say I blame Tasha for going after Gavin."

In an attempt to reach the ball, Gavin lunged up, the muscles in his back flexing.

"Neither do I," Courtney admitted.

Even though she trusted Courtney, a hint of possessiveness swept through her and she had to bite her tongue to keep from telling her cousin to stay away from him.

"But back to my question. Does Gavin live in Providence?"

"No, Manhattan. Why?"

"I've seen him or his twin a few times at Meg's building."

"Are you sure?"

It was a silly question, because Courtney never forgot a face—or much of anything else for that matter. The woman was a literal genius with the IQ to prove it. Regardless, Leah didn't think the man her cousin had seen could be Gavin. When he wasn't traveling for work, he was putting in twelve-plus-hour days at the office.

Courtney looked back over at the group playing volleyball and then at Leah again. "You're really asking me that. Look at him. His not exactly the type you forget."

"Good point," Leah said as she reached for the lemonade she'd brought down. And she was extremely glad she had. Watching Gavin play while dressed in only his shorts was making her hotter than a summer afternoon in Death Valley.

"Does he have any family in Providence?" Courtney asked.

"His mom and stepfather live somewhere in Rhode

Island, but I'm not sure where. He has a stepbrother in the area too."

"Who is his mom?"

"Faith Williamson."

"Really? I didn't know that. He doesn't look anything like her." Courtney turned her attention back to the friendly game on the sand. "Anyway, I've seen him or someone who looks like him going into the apartment next to Meg's, and it doesn't belong to his mom. I've never talked to the woman who lives there, but I've seen her a couple times when I've gone to see Meg. She looks about our age."

Leah considered her cousin's words. Gavin had never once mentioned traveling to Providence or anywhere else to visit friends, and his sister Vivian lived in California. Besides, the only travel he seemed to do was for work.

"Have you seen him there recently?"

Courtney swallowed her mouthful of lemonade and set the glass down. "Last Friday. It was Meg's turn again to host book club."

"He must have a doppelganger running around. Gavin was in Mississippi last week on business." At least she hoped so, because if not Gavin had lied to her. While friends didn't have to tell each other everything, she saw no good reason for him to lie about his whereabouts last week or any other time.

Unless he has something to hide.

She watched Trent high-five Gavin after he spiked the ball over the net and Jake failed to return it. After the kisses they'd shared today, she'd never see him as just a friend again. Before she got in any deeper and risked getting burned a third time, she needed to know she could trust him. Confronting him would be awkward, but what other choice did she have?

THE FIRST VOLLEY of fireworks exploded, filling the night sky with color. Every Fourth of July, Leah looked forward to the dazzling show. Until her conversation with Courtney, today hadn't been any different, but since their chat on the beach her mood had deteriorated. Rather than enjoy the party and time with her family, she spent the afternoon considering the best way to question Gavin when they finally got a moment alone. She didn't want to accuse him of anything when it was possible the person Courtney saw wasn't even him. Unfortunately, she couldn't shake the uneasy feeling the man her cousin had seen was Gavin. And as much as she cared about him, she wasn't going to be the other woman for him or anyone else.

Gavin's hand closed around hers, jolting her from thoughts of the conversation they needed to have. "I never told anyone this, but when I was a kid fireworks petrified me."

"They are loud. You wouldn't be the first child to be afraid of them," she said.

He moved closer on the blanket they were sharing. "It wasn't the sound. I was afraid the sparks would fall around me and set everything on fire." Gavin raised her hand toward his lips. "Stupid, I know, but at the time it seemed possible." His breath washed over her skin as he spoke, and then he kissed her knuckles.

With everyone watching the display in the sky, they could leave and no one would notice. As much as she loved fireworks, she needed to get to the bottom of this mystery so she could hopefully go back to enjoying her time with Gavin.

"Not stupid at all." Leah turned her gaze from the sky toward him. "Do you mind coming inside with me?"

"No, but you want to go now? The fireworks just started." His voice reflected his surprise. Considering the beautiful display overhead, she understood, but she could no longer wait to get this cleared up.

Leah pulled her hand away and came to her feet. "If we go now, no one will bother us." She slipped her sandals back on and waited.

Gavin didn't argue. Standing, he reached for her hand again. "Lead the way."

She didn't expect anyone to come inside anytime soon, but regardless, she brought Gavin through the house and to the small living room. Unlike the larger, more formal one her parents used when entertaining, this room was only used by family members. After switching on the lights, she closed the door just in case someone wandered down the hall and got nosy.

Leah leaned against the door. "You're probably going to think I've lost it," she said as he started toward her. Getting right to the point seemed the best strategy. "But Courtney said she saw you last weekend when she was visiting a friend. Were you in Providence, or do you have a doppelgänger running around?"

HE'D PLANNED on telling her about Erin soon, but not tonight. Unfortunately, he had no other choice now. Sure, he could tell Leah the man her cousin had seen wasn't him, but that would mean lying to her. Lies, no matter how big or small, had a way of coming back to haunt you.

"Actually, Courtney said she's seen you or your identical twin going into an apartment at the Mayfair other times too," Leah continued, not giving him a chance to answer.

"I was there, but I didn't see Courtney." He reached for Leah's hand, but she jerked it away before he could take it. Clasping her hands behind her back, she moved away from the door and him. The gesture hurt more than a slap to the face.

"Why did you tell me you were in Jackson if you were in Providence? I'm not your keeper. You can go anywhere you want."

She was trying to act as if she didn't care, but he heard the truth in her voice. And he wished he'd told her about his regular trips to Providence long before tonight. "I was in Jackson for a week. When I finished up there, I flew to Rhode Island and spent two nights in Providence. I got back to New York late Sunday night, like I told you."

Hoping she'd join him, Gavin moved to the sofa and sat. "I know what you're thinking, Leah, and you're wrong."

"Oh really? And just what am I thinking?" she asked, glaring at him.

Wrong choice of words. Until this moment, the only time he'd seen her mad was the day she caught Harry with another woman.

"Sorry, I didn't mean it the way it sounded. If you'll give me a chance, I can explain why your cousin has seen me at the Mayfair."

Leah sat at the other end of the sofa, as far away from him as she could get and still be on the same piece of furniture. "I'm listening."

"My daughter lives in Providence with her mom. I have an—"

She waved her hands in the air, her eyes the size of dessert plates. "Whoa, wait a minute. Daughter? You have a daughter? Since when?"

Shock beat anger in his book. He only hoped the anger didn't return when the shock wore off. "Erin's nine. She'll be ten in the fall. Her mom and I met in graduate school, but it didn't work out. Our relationship ended not long after Erin was born. Two years ago, Amber accepted a position in Rhode Island, and they moved there."

Leah rubbed both hands down her face. "Sorry, I'm trying to digest all this." Standing, she took a few steps away from the sofa before stopping and shaking her head. Then she turned and faced him again. "You have a daughter and that's who you were visiting when Courtney saw you."

He nodded, wishing he'd told Leah about Erin long before tonight. "If it was on Friday, I was picking Erin up. I have a place in Providence so I don't waste the time we have together driving back and forth to New York. During the summer and over school vacations when our visits are longer, she comes and stays with me in Manhattan."

"And Amber, your ex-girlfriend, called this morning to tell you she got engaged."

Time to come clean about that too. "Actually, it was Erin who called to tell me. She's down in Florida with Amber and Todd, Amber's boyfriend. She was really excited about getting to be in a wedding and couldn't wait to tell me."

"We've been spending time together for three months, Gavin. Even when I was dating Harry, we hung out together. Why didn't you ever tell me you have a daughter?" Leah asked, sounding both hurt and disappointed but at least not angry.

He understood her experiencing both emotions. Even anger he would understand. "I was a little younger than Erin when Dad met his third wife. Joy formed a relationship with us so Dad would propose. Once she got what she wanted, she didn't want anything else to do with us. Vivian especially was crushed. I never want Erin to be in a similar situation, so I don't tell anyone about her until I know them well," he admitted, and although she might push him away, Gavin walked over to her and put his hands on her shoulders. "And I figured avoiding the topic of my family in general was the best way to keep from reminding you Harry and I are related. We share some of the same DNA, but we're nothing alike. I didn't want you to think I was anything like him or our father." He hadn't told her anything about his dad, but his father's infidelity during his first three marriages was well known.

Some of the tension in Leah's shoulder disappeared, but she kept her hands down by her sides. "I figured out you two are complete opposites when Harry and I were dating, Gavin. A person couldn't spend time with the two of you and not realize it."

"I'm going to take that as a compliment," he joked, hoping to lighten the atmosphere. Leah cracked a smile. "And I planned to tell you about my daughter soon. When Erin gets back, she's going to spend time with me in New York. I want you to meet her."

"Does she have you wrapped around her little finger the same way Reese has my brother?"

She hadn't agreed to meet Erin or to even spend any more time with him. Still, he took the fact Leah hadn't walked away or asked him to leave as a good sign. Pulling her in closer, he pretended to consider her question.

"Worse."

"Worse? This I've got to see," she replied, slipping her arms over his shoulders and clasping her hands behind his neck. "When will she be with you?"

"The end of the month."

"I look forward to getting to know her."

He wanted to tell her how pleased her comment made him. She didn't give him a chance. Before his brain could finish getting the thought to his mouth, she touched her lips to his, sending a jolt of joy straight to his heart.

Sounds in the hallway caught his attention, and although his body was telling him to not let go of her, his mind suggested he end their kiss before someone came inside. It was a difficult decision, but in the end his brain won out.

After pulling away, he brushed one final kiss across Leah's forehead and watched her eyes slowly open. "Sounds like the fireworks are over."

"Yeah, people will be leaving soon." She reached up and brushed her fingers against his cheek.

"And I should too. I still need to check in at my hotel." When he'd booked the room, he mentioned he'd be arriving on the late side. "What time should I come back in the morning?"

"Whenever. Curt's not expecting us until around noon, so whatever works best for you."

What worked best for him was taking her back to his hotel room tonight and waking up with her in the morning. Telling her that was out of the question. "How does ten sound?"

"Perfect," she answered, right before the door opened and Curt poked his head inside the room.

"Sorry for interrupting." Curt's expression suggested he was anything but sorry. "I've been looking for both of you. Reese wants to say goodbye before we leave."

Curt pushed the door open wider and Reese entered. At some point she'd changed into pajamas, and she was holding a stuffed tiger. Despite the late hour and the busy day she'd had, the girl didn't look tired at all. When Erin had a day as full of activity as Reese's had been, she looked the same way when the fun came to an end. Then she'd insist she wasn't tired—at least until she finally sat down long enough and then sleep usually took over. Gavin had a feeling the same would happen once Reese was sitting inside Curt's car.

Reese said goodnight to them both before dashing back out the door in search of Leah's parents.

"See you both tomorrow," Curt said before walking away and leaving the door wide open.

"A little protective?" he asked, even though the answer was already crystal clear to him.

Since Vivian and he were the same age, he didn't act the protective brother often. Yes, he gave her his opinion about the guys she got involved with, but it rarely went much further than that. With his younger sister, Piper, it'd be a different story. When the time came for her to start dating, a concept that already set his nerves on edge, he'd be acting much more like Leah's brother. Probably even worse, considering the age gap between him and Piper. Forget about it when Erin was old enough to date. Already he was considering locking her up in a tower like a princess from one of her favorite fairy tales when the time came.

Leah rolled her eyes. "Sometimes, but for some crazy reason I still love him. Don't worry, I'll make sure he behaves tomorrow."

He wasn't worried about her brother or anyone else in her family. Gavin was worried that after she had some time to think about it, she'd reconsider her apparent willingness to forgive him for keeping Erin a secret all this time.

"Promise?" Even though the door remained open, he couldn't keep from brushing a kiss across her lips.

"Absolutely."

Bits and pieces of conversations drifted into the room as people passed the door. Before another family member or guest interrupted them, he took a step away from her.

He didn't ask her to, but Leah walked him outside. Despite other guests being around, he couldn't resist giving her one last kiss before getting in his car and driving away.

With several projects still needing his attention, he'd brought along his laptop this morning. After checking into his room at the Sherbrooke Hotel on America's Cup Avenue, he ordered a pot of coffee and an order of loaded nachos from room service before getting down to work. Countless times, both Leah and his sister had referred to him as a workaholic. Although he never thought of himself that way, he couldn't deny much of his time was spent working. If he hoped to have a relationship with Leah, he needed to find a way to get the same amount accomplished and still have time for her, which meant he saw a lot of sleepless nights in his future. In his opinion, having Leah in his life was worth much more than some missed sleep.

FIVE

Leah watched the waves crashing against the beach. She'd been up for well over two hours, but rather than get dressed and search out any family members who might be downstairs, she slipped on a bathrobe and stepped onto the balcony. Although the beach remained empty, she could picture Gavin sitting on the sand as they helped Reese build her mega sandcastle. The thing really had been enormous by the time they finished it. And not once while they worked had Gavin showed an ounce of annoyance as the little girl chatted away. Boy, did she chat too.

As the memories of Gavin and Reese interacting played through her thoughts, Leah realized she hadn't asked him if he had any pictures of his daughter. None of her friends had children, but several of her cousins did. They all had numerous photos of their children stored on their cell phones. Most likely Gavin did too, and she was more than a little curious about what Erin looked like. Did she have Gavin's dark eyes and hair or did she take after his ex-girlfriend? At the thought of Amber, a slight wave of jealousy passed through her. Intellectually she knew it was unwarranted.

They'd not only broken up years ago, but Amber lived almost two hundred miles away from Gavin and was engaged to another man. Still, the idea of Gavin having a child with some faceless woman annoyed her. She wondered if her cousin's girlfriend, Paige, ever experienced similar emotions. While it was clear to anyone with eyes that Scott was head over heels in love with Paige, he did have an eleven-month-old son from a previous relationship. If it did bother Paige, she never showed it. Whenever Leah saw her with Scott's son, Paige treated Cooper like he was her own child.

He's a dad. For the umpteenth time the words went through her head as she stepped back inside her bedroom.

"Gavin has a nine-year-old daughter."

Never in a million years would she have guessed. While it didn't change her feelings for Gavin or her desire to see where things between them went, the fact he'd kept the truth from her despite all the time they'd spent together stung.

"His reasons make some sense," she said to her reflection in the mirror as she pulled shorts and a top from a drawer. There was a lot about her private life that she only shared after she knew a person well. Not to mention, if she had a brother and a father with reputations similar to Harry's and Mr. Kincaid's, she wouldn't want to talk about her family either and have people believe she was anything like them—especially a man she was interested in dating.

She carried the clean clothes into her private bathroom and turned on the shower. Leah knew the truth now, so there was no point in dwelling on the fact he'd waited months to tell her. Nope, instead she'd enjoy the day with him as well as her brother, his girlfriend, and Reese. Maybe in the process she'd get to the bottom of how Curt and Reese had become so close in a rather short period of time. She could see it happening if Reese was Taylor's daughter, but she wasn't. So there had to be a story there.

Then later today when they were alone, she fully expected to be on the receiving end of Gavin's kisses. She'd gone on her first date at fifteen, so she'd kissed her share of men, however never had a kiss hit her the way his did. She'd read in novels that a character got weak in the knees during a kiss and until last night she'd thought it was a silly description authors used. Thanks to Gavin, she knew the expression existed for a reason.

If he's that good at kissing, how is he at other things?

She'd never been one to lounge around and fantasize about sex, but the image of them together in her bed sprang to life as she stepped under the hot water.

Hold your horses. We kissed a few times. That's a long way from making love.

Squeezing her eyes shut, Leah forced the oh-so-delightful picture from her mind and lathered the soap between her hands. She didn't care if it had been almost ten months since she had sex. Before she let him in her bed or jumped into his for that matter, she needed things to grow between them. Only once had she slept with a guy less than a week after getting into a relationship with him. About four months in to their relationship, she'd learned Benedict, her boyfriend before Harry, was seeing another woman. A woman he married about a month after Leah dumped him and then divorced less than a year later. And she hadn't slept with anyone including Harry since.

This time around she planned to take it slow, because while she knew Gavin far better than she'd known either of her last two boyfriends, there was still a lot she didn't know, like whether he preferred his eggs scrambled or over easy or if he'd played any sports in high school. There was a lot he didn't know about her too. This afternoon she'd work to rectify both.

WHEN LEAH finally made her way downstairs, she found her cousin, his wife, and their son enjoying a late breakfast on the deck. Normally when Jake and his family visited Newport, they stayed at Cliff House, his father's home. With the home's interior being painted, they'd opted to stay with Leah's parents instead this weekend.

"Nice bit of rescuing yesterday. I could've used someone like you when Tasha was after me," Jake said once Leah was settled across the table from him.

Him too? "Did everyone see us on the deck?"

Courtney, Trent, and Derek had all made sure to comment on the brief encounter between Gavin, Tasha, and her yesterday afternoon.

Jake caught the sippy cup his son knocked off the table before it hit the ground. "Doubt it." He placed the cup back on the table. "The little scene on the beach, though, everyone saw."

Not much embarrassed her, but heat filled her face at Jake's comment. Had everyone at the party seen them kissing?

"Stop tormenting her." Charlie nudged Jake with her elbow and then turned her attention Leah's way. "Neither of us saw anything. Your brother has a big mouth and told Jake. I think most people were too busy eating to notice you two."

Leah hoped Charlie wasn't only saying that to make her feel better.

"And he shouldn't have told you, Jake," Charlie added.

She agreed wholeheartedly.

"Why didn't you bring Gavin to Gray's wedding?" Jake asked.

Because I was too much of an idiot to realize I cared about him as more than a friend.

"He wasn't around." She didn't feel like explaining how their relationship had taken a sudden turn yesterday, and besides, it wasn't a lie. Before Jake could pursue the topic, she changed the subject.

"Do you know if Sara and Christopher are coming out this way soon?" she asked, refilling her iced tea from the pitcher on the table.

Jake added another blueberry muffin to his plate before he spoke. "Last time I talked to her, they planned on coming next month." He broke the muffin in half and had it almost to his month before he stopped. "You've got company." He gestured toward the door behind her with his chin.

She turned in her seat. "Morning," she greeted. Leah allowed herself a moment to soak in his appearance, and the memory of him playing volleyball without a shirt rushed forward. She needed to put some thought into how she might be able to get the gray T-shirt he wore now off at some point before the day ended.

Before exchanging pleasantries with either Jake or Charlie, Gavin kissed her cheek and then sat in the empty chair next to her.

"Nice to see you both again," Gavin commented before yawning.

"Someone needs caffeine." She'd had her fair share already since waking up. The iced tea in her hand was her fourth since getting out of bed. "Do you want a coffee or an iced tea?"

Rubbing his eyes, he shook his head. "My stomach can't handle any more caffeine right now. Room service delivered a pot of coffee this morning, and I drank the entire thing. Maybe later."

"Only one? You're a lightweight," Jake jokingly tossed out. "I had twice as much before I showered today."

She'd never seen anyone ingest more coffee than Jake and

his wife. She'd watched him finish one cup already, and who knew how many he had before she joined him, so it was quite possible he wasn't exaggerating about the amount he drank before getting showered.

"It was a big pot," Gavin offered.

"Sure it was," Jake teased.

Gavin might not realize it, but her cousin's teasing was Jake's way of letting her know he liked the guy. Although not 100 percent accurate, more times than not when Jake and the other male members of her family liked someone she dated, it was a good sign. No one who had met Benedict or Harry liked either of them. Those relationships had turned out to be the two worst she'd ever had.

"What are your plans for the day? Charlie and I are taking the boat out for a few hours. Aunt Judith promised to watch Garrett while we're gone. You're welcome to join us."

"Promised? More like insisted," Charlie said. "I get the impression she's anxious for grandchildren."

Charlie's comment was spot-on. Ever since Uncle Warren's first grandchild had been born, Mom had been saying how much she was looking forward to becoming a grandmother some day. Since she had none yet, every chance Mom got she spoiled the four little boys who'd been born to Leah's various cousins instead.

"You should come. It'll be fun," Charlie added.

She'd gone sailing more times than she could count with Jake on the sailboat he kept moored at Cliff House. If they didn't already have plans with Curt, she'd have accepted. Or maybe not. Now that she thought about it, she didn't know if Gavin enjoyed being out on the water or not. It was another one of those things they'd never discussed. For all she knew, he might get deathly seasick every time he stepped on a boat.

"Thanks, but Curt invited us over," Leah replied.

"Wish you'd asked sooner. I haven't been sailing in a couple years," Gavin replied.

Answers that question. Gavin might not enjoy being on the water as much as she did, but he liked it enough to want to go today.

"I'd say we should do it tomorrow, but we're heading up to North Salem in the morning." Jake drained the liquid in his mug and reached for the coffee carafe on the table.

Both Charlie's mom and older brother still lived in North Salem, and they tried to visit as often as possible.

Jake poured more coffee into both his and Charlie's mugs before adding cream and sugar to his and mixing it. "We should be around again before the summer ends and the boat goes into dry dock. Let's plan on going then."

It might be jumping the gun to make any future plans for them, but she didn't care. If something came up between now and then, she could cancel. Jake wouldn't take it personally. "Just call and let us know when you'll be here."

"Curt invited you over." Jake's smile told everyone who knew him that he was headed back into teasing mode again. "Hope you're ready for an old-fashioned interrogation, Gavin, because he's got one planned for you. And in case you're wondering, he's good at it."

"Knock it off, Jake." Charlie gave him a slight nudge with her elbow again.

"What? It's true. He's almost as good as I am."

Leah and Charlie glanced at each and rolled their eyes at the same time. "Charlie, I'm glad you're the one who has to live with him."

Eventually Leah's mom and dad joined them. They planned to spend the next week in Newport like they always did at this time of year, and for the second time that weekend, Mom invited Leah to stay an extra couple of days. A month ago she would've accepted and enjoyed some long overdue time with her parents. As the only girl in the family, she'd always had an extra-special bond with her mom. Unfortunately, with her parents living in Massachusetts and her in Connecticut, they didn't see each other as often as Leah would like. This week would've been a perfect time to correct that, but with this new development between her and Gavin, she didn't want to remain here while he went back to Manhattan.

On an average day, the drive from her parents' home to Curt's beach house took five minutes. With so many tourists adding to the traffic in Newport, it took them almost fifteen minutes to reach her brother's place.

Since her brother had left the front door open, Leah didn't bother to ring the doorbell, she just walked in. It'd been a year since she'd visited the house, but it looked unchanged. Although the living room was empty, the glass doors leading outside were open, and she could see Reese and Curt playing checkers at the table while Taylor sat nearby. It was a scene perfect for a family photo.

"I should've asked you last night. Do you have any pictures of Erin?" With her family around earlier, it had seemed like the wrong time to ask if Gavin had any photos of Erin with him. Before Curt noticed them, she wanted her curiosity appeased.

Gavin pulled his cell phone from his back pocket. "There might be one or two on here." He thumbed on the device and opened an app before handing it to her. "I took these last weekend when we went to Roger Williams Park. Her two favorite things to do there are visiting the botanical center and watching the elephants get a bath."

Calling it a park was misleading. She'd visited a few times as a child and knew Roger Williams Park included a large zoo, a museum of natural history, a carousel, a bandstand, a botanical center, and numerous manicured gardens. A person could spend an entire day there and not see everything it offered.

She accepted the cell phone. The image of a smiling, dark-haired girl who was missing one of her bottom teeth filled the screen. A large giraffe occupied the background, telling Leah the picture had been taken inside the zoo.

"She looks like you." She didn't know what Erin's mom looked like, but Leah didn't see anyone but Gavin in the young girl's face.

She scrolled through some of the other pictures on the device. Most were of Erin alone. There were a few of Erin and Gavin's younger half sister, Piper, who most would assume was Erin's cousin because of the closeness in age. There were a few of Erin with Gavin's twin, Vivian, as well. Finally she came across one of Gavin and Erin together. He held a pair of skis, and both were dressed for a day on the slopes. She'd never cared much for skiing. She'd learned because her parents sent her and her brothers for lessons, but she'd preferred sitting in the warm lodge drinking hot chocolate to being out in the cold snow. Her brothers had been the opposite. They never wanted to come in, and whenever the family went skiing, Curt and Brett would spend the entire day out on the slopes, only coming inside when they needed to eat or when the slopes closed for the night.

"Where was this one taken?" She turned the device in his direction so he could see the picture.

GAVIN REMEMBERED EXACTLY when the photo of him and Erin had been taken. Every year he made it a point to take Erin skiing a few times, but the picture on the screen had been taken the first time she'd tried snowboarding. She'd bugged him to try the previous year, but, worried it'd be too dangerous, he'd made her wait until she was nine.

"Up at Stratton Mountain in February over school break. We both love to ski, but this year she tried snowboarding. This one was taken right after her first lesson. I had trouble getting her off the mountain again that day. Finally an empty stomach got her inside."

He scrolled through a few more pictures. When he found the one he wanted, he handed the phone back to her. "I took this one the same day but several hours later."

Despite her insistence she wasn't tired, Erin had fallen asleep while eating and he hadn't been able to resist snapping a picture of her asleep at the table, an entire slice of pizza on her plate mere inches from her lips.

"I knew she wouldn't believe me if I told her she fell asleep sitting there. She didn't make a sound when I carried her to bed and tucked her in."

"And what did she say in the morning?"

"She denied falling asleep during dinner." He pointed to the photo still on the screen. "Until I showed her this, anyway."

When Leah gave him back the phone, he shoved it into his pocket again.

Smiling, she took his hand. "I can't wait to meet her."

And he couldn't wait to introduce her to Erin.

Focused on the checkerboard on the table, no one looked up when they stepped outside. Curt's lack of attention wouldn't last. Leah's cousin might have been exaggerating earlier about Curt interrogating him, but Gavin expected the guy to keep a close eye on him today.

"King me," Reese called out happily after moving her red checker over one of Curt's black ones and into an empty square.

Curt obliged and looked up at his two guests. "Make yourself at home. We're almost done here. Reese is crushing me today." Leah's brother went back to studying the board.

Gavin glanced at the game. If Curt wanted to he could easily catch up and perhaps win. If he could see that, Leah's brother could too. Rather than make the move that would even up the game, Curt went with a different one—one that put him in a decent position but didn't give him the edge the other move would've.

"Curt, are you sure you want to do that?" Leah asked before Reese took her turn.

"Yeah, why?" Curt inquired, looking up from the board.

"Because there's a better move you can make," she answered, taking a seat at the table.

"We can't get help from others," Reese informed Leah.

Gavin cleared his throat in an effort not to laugh. The girl sounded extremely serious.

"Sorry, I didn't know," Leah apologized, her lips trying not to break into a smile. "I won't say anything else to him. Can I play the winner?"

"Auntie Taylor is going to, but maybe you can play the winner from that game."

"Leah, the checkers are all yours. Reese and I play a lot at home. I don't mind sitting out for a round," Taylor replied.

He and Erin played all the classic board games as well as a few new ones, but they'd never played checkers. He wasn't even sure she knew how. He already had a chessboard, but when he got home he'd pick up a set of checkers. Then the next time they were looking for a game to play, they could give it a try. As a kid, he'd enjoyed playing against both Harry and Vivian. Most of the time he won, especially against Harry, which was probably why his half brother often tried to cheat.

THE GAME between Leah and Reese ended up being a close

one, but in the end one bad move on Leah's part handed the little girl the win. Following the game, Taylor agreed to one final match against her niece. Much to Reese's disappointment, she didn't win the game against her aunt. Afterward she cleaned up the game before heading down to play in the sand, leaving the adults to engage in conversation while still keeping an eye on her.

"Curt, I love your stuffed animal collection sitting on the sofa," Leah teased.

At least twenty different stuffed toys were carefully arranged on the sofa inside. The sight of the colorful toys reminded Gavin of how Erin insisted on arranging each of her own stuffies just so on her bed.

Opening the cover for the grill, Curt took the comment in stride. "My secret's out. But that collection is nothing compared to the one I have in New Hampshire."

"Well, when it's time to pick out a birthday present for you, I know just what to get," Leah said.

Curt removed the burgers and sausages from the grill's surface before lowering the cover. "If you can find it, I'd love a purple and pink unicorn for my collection. Or a fuzzy panda bear. I've always wanted a panda bear to sleep with at night."

Reese, who joined them reluctantly after her aunt called her up, giggled as she sat down. "Grown-ups don't have stuffies."

"Who says we don't, short stuff?" Curt added the platter to the already overflowing table of food. "I bet Gavin has a whole closet full."

The girl laughed again, an infectious sound that had him chuckling too. "He does not," Reese insisted. She didn't wait for anyone else to grab food before adding a burger to her plate. "Stuffed animals are for kids."

"I've got one at home in my closet. It's a dark gray cat named Mr. Floppy." Leah entered the conversation.

"You still have Mr. Floppy? I'm surprised it survived this long. You used to take that stuffed cat everywhere. Mom was always afraid you'd leave it somewhere," Curt commented.

Gavin could relate. When Erin was younger, she wouldn't leave the house without her favorite elephant and doll. She still insisted on bringing them with her when she visited him and slept with them every night, but they didn't make anymore trips to the movie theater or park.

"Why did you name it Mr. Floppy? That doesn't sound like a cat's name. It sounds like a bunny's name," Reese asked before squirting a puddle of ketchup on her burger.

Reese had a point. Mr. Floppy did sound like a good name for a stuffed bunny rabbit with long ears. Then again, he'd had a favorite bear as a little kid. Even though it had been all white, he'd called it Brownie. According to Mom, he named it that because at the time his favorite food was brownies, a sweet treat he still preferred over ice cream or cookies.

"His arms and legs were extra floppy and soft," Leah explained. "They're still floppy but not very soft anymore. Most of the fur on them is gone from being washed so many times."

Gradually the conversation moved away from stuffed animals to baseball. Having grown up along the New York/Connecticut border, he'd always been a New York fan. He might prefer the New England Rebels when it came to football, but when it came to baseball, nothing would ever make him a Boston fan. Unfortunately, like most New Englanders living anywhere east of Hartford, Connecticut, everyone else at the table hated New York. It didn't bother him. He was just happy Leah liked baseball. Amber hated it. When they'd been together, she refused to go to games with him. The few women he'd dated since hadn't shown any interest in it either. Since she never mentioned it, he'd expected Leah to be the same.

"The next time New York plays Boston, we should all go together," Leah suggested. "I'm sure they'll face each other a few more times before the season ends."

"Can I come too?" Reese asked around a mouthful of food. "I've never been to a baseball game. Curt took me to see a soccer game for my birthday. It's my favorite sport. I'm teaching him how to play, and he's teaching me how to play lacrosse. I want to try out for the team next year."

Leah didn't need to say anything for Gavin to know what she was thinking. She'd shared her curiosity regarding Reese and Curt's relationship yesterday. These comments would only intensify it. He hoped Leah got to the bottom of the mystery soon, because even he was curious.

"She's a tough coach." Curt added more potato salad to his plate before grabbing a burger and stacking pickles and tomatoes on it.

"Those are often the best kinds. One of my favorite coaches in high school was also my toughest, but I learned the most from him," Gavin shared.

"Did you play soccer?" Reese asked, licking a blob of ketchup that had dripped out of her burger off her finger, something both Erin and Piper would do without a second thought. They, like most children, loved ketchup. He didn't understand how anyone ate the stuff. Even as a kid he'd hated it. But Erin and Piper added it to almost everything. He even once caught Erin putting it on her pancakes.

"Yep. That and basketball. I started when I was around your age and played until college. My daughter plays too." Since Leah knew about Erin, he didn't need to keep silent about her any longer.

The mustard bottle Curt had picked up slipped from his

hand and landed in the bowl of chips. He didn't bother to retrieve it.

"You have a daughter?" Curt's gaze swung in Leah's direction. "Did you know Gavin has a daughter?"

Perhaps taking pity on her brother, Leah fished the mustard bottle from the chips and held it toward him. "Yes. She looks just like him."

"What position did you play?" Reese asked, oblivious to the look Curt was sending his sister's way. "I'm usually a striker, but sometimes my coach makes me play defense. Once he made me play goalie. I didn't like it, and I hope he doesn't make me do it again."

In the beginning Erin had hated playing goalie too, until she realized how important a position it was. "I started playing goalie in sixth grade. It's a critical position."

Reese didn't look convinced. "Coach Simon told me that too. Maybe we can all play after lunch." She looked expectantly at each of the adults seated at the table.

"I'm up for a game." He never turned down an opportunity to play soccer or basketball. "Leah?"

"I haven't played since gym class in school, but I'll try."

"Auntie Taylor played soccer like me. Did you play sports when you were a kid?" Reese asked before sinking her teeth into her burger.

Good question. He pictured Leah as more of a dancer, but if she enjoyed watching sports, perhaps she'd played them as well.

"I played field hockey; it's similar to soccer. And I danced," Leah answered.

"My best friend Hazel dances. She wants me to do it with her, but I don't want to. It's boring."

Reese would get along very well with his daughter. Unless she was dancing in her bedroom, she felt the same way about dance, much to Amber's dismay. She'd danced competitively and wanted their daughter to love it as much as she did.

"Have you ever tried it?" Leah asked.

He'd worried she'd be uncomfortable around Erin when they finally met, but all day yesterday and again today she'd seemed comfortable interacting with Reese.

"Auntie Taylor signed me up once for ballet. It was awful, and I had to wear tights."

"Ballet can be a little slow compared to other styles. Maybe you'd like jazz or hip-hop. Dance can be a lot of fun."

Reese looked unconvinced as she added another spoonful of potato salad to her plate. Gavin didn't blame her. Vivian had danced, and he still remembered sitting through the painfully boring recitals. If Erin decided to give dance another try, he'd go and watch, but honestly he was happy she'd given up after her first year. She hadn't even made it to the end of her first year. About two months before her recital, with her costumes in the closet, she quit and she never asked to try it again.

USING the ruse that she intended to help her brother get the dessert ready, Leah left Gavin, Taylor, and Reese on the beach kicking around a soccer ball. Although it wasn't any of her business, she wanted answers to questions she didn't want to ask in front of Curt's girlfriend or Reese.

"Need any help?" Leah called out, entering the large open kitchen.

At the counter, Curt transferred the most delicious-looking cupcakes she'd ever seen onto a serving plate. A large fruit torte was out of its box and waiting to be served next to it.

"Couldn't keep up with Reese?" He set the last cupcake

on the plate and then licked the frosting off his finger. Then after washing his hands, he went to the fridge and pulled out another pastry box.

"She does seem to have an endless supply of energy." Leah pulled out a barstool at the counter and sat. "Is she always like that?"

"Yep. She's either on full speed or sleeping. She doesn't have a middle setting."

"You two seem close. Does Taylor babysit her a lot?"

Curt shook his head as he took an éclair from the box. After tearing it in half, he handed her part of the tasty treat. "Taylor is Reese's guardian. She has been since Reese was a baby."

Her brother's statement explained so much. Taylor was more or less the girl's mother. "How old was Reese when her mom died?"

It seemed like a logical question. Why else would Taylor be Reese's guardian? The sudden anger that swept over Curt's face told a different story.

"Eliza isn't dead. Right now she's in jail, and hopefully she'll spend the rest of her life there."

Leah shivered at Curt's frigid tone, and considering his reaction, she wasn't going to ask any more questions. If he wanted to share more, he would. "Well, she's a sweet girl and seems to adore you."

"What about Gavin's daughter? Do you two get along?"

She decided now was as good a time as any to sample the half of the éclair Curt handed her. So rather than answer, Leah took a big bite from the custard-filled pastry. "This is awesome. Where did you get them?"

Curt polished off the half he held, then went back to adding the box's contents to a plate. "They opened an Ambrosia in Newport a few months ago. I stopped over there this morning after breakfast."

Leah was familiar with the family-owned pastry shop and café based out of Providence. "I wish they'd open one near me. I'd be there every other day. Did you get any of their cannoli?" She'd yet to find a bakery that made better cannoli than Ambrosia.

"Not today, and back to my question, which you so nicely ignored."

Why did I bother? Ignoring one of Curt's questions and hoping he'd forget about it was pointless.

"We haven't met. She lives in Providence with her mom and usually Gavin goes there to see her."

"And?" he prompted.

"And what?" Leah asked, focusing on the selection of desserts before her rather than Curt.

"There's more to the story. I hear it in your voice, Leah."

Her brother could be too perceptive on occasion. "Until yesterday I didn't know Gavin had a daughter."

Curt made a sound of disapproval. "A child is something he should've told you about before yesterday. I assume he had a good excuse." He leaned back against the opposite counter.

"I wish he'd told me sooner too, but I understand his reasons."

"As along as you're okay with it, that's what matters. Gavin seems like a good guy, but be careful. If he kept a daughter a secret this long, he might have other ones too."

Leah appreciated and understood her brother's concern. "True. He might snore like a bear." She picked up the platter of cupcakes. "If we stay in here any longer, I'm going to eat all of these."

Pushing off the counter, he took the other two plates of treats, but he didn't move any farther. "When the two of you have the time, come up and visit me. You still haven't seen the new house. I've made a lot of progress. And you can meet Taylor's mom. She lives with Taylor and Reese."

Dragging Gavin away for a day or so to visit her brother might be tough. It was a good thing she liked a challenge. "I'm dying to see what kind of mess you've picked up this time. We'll be around soon."

SIX

Rolling over, Leah opened her eyes and gazed up at the ceiling. Judging by the amount of sunlight in the room, it was still early. Sometimes she didn't know why she bothered setting an alarm when she stayed at her apartment in the city. No matter what time she went to bed, she always woke up long before she needed to. The same thing happened whenever she traveled, regardless of whether it was for business or pleasure. She assumed it was because she wasn't sleeping in her bed. Well, when she stayed at her place in the city, it was technically her bed, but not her normal bed. In fact, it wasn't uncommon for weeks to go by between her visits to the apartment, because as much as she loved visiting the city and working there, she much preferred living away from it. Still, she kept the place, located inside one of the Sherbrooke hotels in Manhattan, because some days she didn't feel like dealing with the traffic out to Greenwich. That had been the exact case last night.

She'd had a late afternoon meeting that lasted much longer than it should have. Afterward she visited her cousin

Scott and his girlfriend, although she would've preferred another evening with Gavin. They'd seen each other every day since the previous Saturday except for one. Bright and early yesterday morning, he'd driven out to Maine and had spent much of the day there. Even though she didn't see him, she had talked to him. Per her request, he'd called when he got back to the city around eleven so she knew he'd made it home safely.

Thankfully, today was Saturday and she had a whole weekend with him to look forward to again. Gavin hadn't shared any details other than to say he had plans for them, and she hadn't pressed the issue because unlike some people, she enjoyed surprises. It didn't mean she hadn't spent the past two days guessing what he had in store for them.

Regardless of what it was, she expected to enjoy herself because in the week they'd been together, he'd been the perfect boyfriend. Despite his over-the-top work ethic, he was attentive and at the same time not overbearing. Plenty of times in the past she'd dated men who all but wanted to put a tracking device on her so they knew exactly where she was at all times when they weren't together.

Leah grabbed her phone and scrolled through her various playlists. She knew from experience that falling back to sleep was out of the question. At the same time, she had zero desire to get out of bed and do anything productive. Losing herself in a book while she listened to music seemed like the ideal way to pass a few hours.

She'd always loved music regardless of the type or the era it came from. She had playlists consisting of everything from songs made popular during the British invasion in the mid-1960s and hits from the hair bands of the 1980s to pieces written by composers such as Mozart and Beethoven. When she'd been younger, her brothers loved teasing her about some of her music choices, especially when she played Frank

Sinatra or Dean Martin. They'd remind her both were singers their grandmother loved, as if that somehow diminished the fabulous voices the two men had.

This morning she selected the playlist consisting of symphonies written by Mozart and his contemporaries. After pressing play, she moved into an upright position and grabbed the e-reader she kept in her nightstand for mornings such as this. She had another one by her bed in Greenwich, so no matter where she stayed she could read whenever she wanted.

After powering on the device, she opened to the eighth chapter in *Fatal Deception*. Recently she'd decided to reread Curt's debut novel because she'd gone through it so fast the first time around she'd missed subtle details—details Gavin had brought to her attention the evening they'd discussed the book over dinner.

Was that really only a week ago?

Rather than start reading, she thought back. Yep, it had definitely been less than two weeks ago. They'd talked about the novel and Gavin's prediction as to what would happen next based on the clues he'd picked up the same night she'd invited him to her parents' party—an invitation he'd accepted with far less resistance than she'd expected. At the time she'd wondered why, but considering the turn their relationship had taken on the beach, she now suspected she understood. And it had definitely taken a turn the moment she slipped her arm around his waist.

Or had it?

True, in the very beginning she'd viewed him as nothing more than a friend, someone to meet for dinner or play golf with. Back then she'd even toyed with the idea of playing Cupid and setting him up with one of her cousins. And like a strictly platonic friend, she hadn't cared whom he spent time with or whether a woman flirted with him when they were out together.

Leah didn't know the precise moment, but she couldn't deny that at some point long before her parents' party something had shifted. She'd lost count of how many times she'd seen a woman flirt with Gavin or even simply send him a suggestive look and she'd gotten annoyed.

In fact, the very night she invited him to Newport for the Fourth of July, she had to remind herself that they were merely friends each time the waitress came over and did everything she could to catch his attention. And she really had done everything, including giving him her phone number, not that Leah had seen the waitress slip it to him. Gavin had shared the annoying detail as they walked to their cars after dinner, and when he did, the desire to demand he tear it up before they left the parking lot had all but choked her. Somehow she managed to keep the words from spilling out. Of course, it'd helped when Gavin admitted he'd left the note behind on the table because he wasn't interested.

Leah considered herself an observant individual, yet somehow despite the emotional clues she'd experienced, she'd missed the writing on the wall. It had taken Gavin's run-in with Tasha, of all people, to set her straight. The moment she'd seen Tasha standing so close wearing her *I'm on the hunt* expression, her emotions took over, and she'd moved in to protect what her subconscious evidently already considered hers.

She might not consider Tasha her favorite person in the world, but she definitely owed her one for giving her the proverbial kick in the pants she'd obviously needed. Too bad she couldn't send the other woman a box of chocolates or some flowers with a thank-you note attached. Although she'd never in a million years do it, Leah considered the wording for such a card.

Dear Tasha, thanks so much for making me jealous last

weekend. Without your help, I'd still have my head in the sand.

Yep, such a message would sum up her sentiments well.

Turning her attention back to the novel, she started on the first paragraph of the chapter. Memories from their walk on the beach after leaving Tasha pushed their way forward before she'd made it past the third sentence.

She'd only realized the transformation in her feelings last weekend, but when had things shifted for him? Had it hit him over the head the night she invited him to the party? Or had he realized it months ago?

She hadn't analyzed their conversation before or after their first kiss. Now she wanted to. Leah tossed aside the e-reader and thought back. She might not be a genius like her cousin and able to remember every minute detail, but she didn't forget much, especially when it pertained to significant events. Their time on the beach certainly qualified as being significant.

Leah replayed the afternoon, starting with the moment Gavin thanked her for rescuing him from Tasha. Before they moved from the deck, she'd been certain he wanted to kiss her. Instead of kissing her, he suggested they take a walk. Then before Gavin touched his lips to hers, he said something along the lines of *there is no other place I want to be.*

"And like an idiot I told him I'd been thinking of setting him up with Courtney or Juliette." She shook her head as she remembered that. Really, who said that after they kissed a guy? Evidently ninnies like her did.

"Let it go. It's not the first stupid thing you've ever said, and it won't be your last." But even if it had been a poorly thought-out statement, his response made up for it. He'd made it clear he wasn't interested in someone else. Unfortunately, she'd cut off the rest of his sentence by kissing him.

Back then she hadn't wondered what else he had to say, but now she wished she'd let him finish.

THE DOORMAN OPENED the door as Leah approached. She hadn't been back to Gavin's condo since the night she caught Harry entertaining another woman. Instead, whenever she and Gavin got together they either met somewhere or he came to her house. Occasionally she felt guilty about that, but not guilty enough to risk running into Harry again. Thankfully Gavin had never complained either. Since he always came to her, she'd insisted on meeting him at his place this morning. He agreed with no argument, which she interpreted to mean he planned to get some work in this morning before they set out for the day.

As she crossed the empty lobby toward the elevators, a flashback to her last visit hit her, momentarily stopping her dead in her tracks.

Gavin's nothing like Harry. I have nothing to worry about, she reminded herself as she stepped inside the elevator.

The doors were almost closed when a woman approached, forcing the doors to reopen. It wasn't just any woman either. Leah mentally shook her head as Amy, the redhead she'd found with Harry, joined her for the ride up. Really, what were the odds of her running into the woman today, considering the number of people who lived in the building?

Amy pressed the button for the floor below Gavin, but her attention was focused on Leah. "Did you just move into the building? I thought I'd met everyone who lived here," Amy asked.

"No, I'm just visiting a friend."

"You look familiar. Have we met before?"

In a manner of speaking, yes. "Not exactly," Leah responded. Before she could come up with a nice way of explaining why she looked familiar, Amy snapped her fingers.

"I know. I saw you at Harry Kincaid's. You used to date him," she said, suddenly looking uncomfortable. "I'm so sorry. When he invited me up, I really didn't know he had a girlfriend. If I'd known, I never would've gone."

How did one respond to such an admission? "No need to apologize. It wasn't your fault." At the moment it was the best she could come up with.

The elevator doors opened at Amy's floor, but she didn't immediately exit. "I walked out right after you that day, and I haven't seen the dirtbag since."

She'd called Harry the exact same thing one or two times. Okay, so more like fifty times, but who was counting?

Amy walked away, saving Leah from having to comment.

HE'D PLANNED out the entire weekend under the assumption the weather was going to be nice. At least when he'd checked it Wednesday night there hadn't been a single rain cloud or thunderbolt on his weather app until the middle of next week. The app was telling him a different story now. If it was correct, there was a 60 percent chance of rain starting at five o'clock tonight. Sunday's weather looked even worse. Since the weather was out of his control, he wasn't going to stress about it. Instead he'd focus on making sure they had an enjoyable weekend regardless of whether he had to make some last-minute adjustments.

Shoving the device back into his pocket, Gavin answered the door. He'd waited months to be able to kiss Leah, and now that he finally could, he did it every chance he got. Like now. Before Leah crossed the threshold into the condo, he pulled her in close and lowered his lips to hers.

"I missed you," he admitted when he pulled his mouth away. "I hope you're ready to have me stuck to your side for the next two days."

She smiled up at him and not for the first time he wondered how his half brother could've been so stupid.

"Looking forward to it." She kissed his cheek and then slipped from his embrace so she could enter. "You're never going to believe who I bumped into on my way up."

Gavin opened his mouth to comment, but she waved a hand dismissively in his direction. "Your neighbor Amy. You know, the woman I caught Harry with."

He'd run into Amy once since then. She'd offered up a polite hello but had otherwise avoided eye contact and remained silent during the elevator ride up. He hadn't bothered to coax her into a conversation either.

"She looked embarrassed once she realized where she recognized me from. And she insisted she didn't know Harry was seeing someone before apologizing."

Leah never brought up what had transpired, so he avoided the topic too. Since she mentioned it, he figured it was safe to tell her what happened after she left. "I don't think she did. By the time I got back inside, she'd dressed and then she stormed out after tossing a few insults Harry's way. She never came back while Harry was living here."

"Smart woman." With a slight shake of her head, Leah dropped onto the sofa. "Did you know he tried to get me to take him back? Seriously, what woman or man would take back someone they caught cheating on them? If a person does it once, they'll do it again."

He knew more than one woman who'd done just that. Harry was a charmer. He always had been. People, especially women, had trouble telling him no. The size of his bank account certainly helped too.

Joining her, he slipped an arm over her shoulders. He found it next to impossible to be in the same room with her and not be touching her. "Yeah, I knew he tried. And to answer your question, you'd be surprised how many times he's gotten a woman to give him a second chance. He, unfortunately, takes after our father when it comes to getting what he wants."

"I actually hung up on him during one of his many tries," Leah admitted with a cheerful smile. "Anyway, enough talking about *him*. I know the two of you are related, but I'd rather forget I ever met Harry."

If he'd dated the female equivalent of his half brother, he'd share Leah's sentiments.

"Harry who?" he asked.

"My thoughts exactly." She leaned in and kissed him before asking, "Okay, I'm dying to know what you have planned for us. Are you going to share or do I need to guess?"

He'd intended to tell her what he had planned as soon as she arrived, but having her guess wasn't a bad idea. It'd give him some possibilities of things she would enjoy doing in the future.

"How about we head out and you can guess on the way," he suggested.

The last time he traveled out to the recreational complex located in West Orange, New Jersey, had been back in mid-April. Erin had been staying with him for spring break, and he'd taken the entire week off so they could go on some day trips together. Before she came, Erin made a list of all the things she wanted to do and places she wanted to see while with him. As always when she came to the city, the place she wanted to visit the most was The Metropolitan Museum of Art.

Erin loved art and had for as long as he could remember. The number two activity on her list, however, had been visiting the complex in New Jersey so she could try the zip line and ropes obstacle course there and play a round of mini golf. During their visit, they'd done both and made a quick visit to the zoo, which was also part of the complex. While not as large or, in his opinion, as nice as Roger Williams Zoo, it made for a nice addition to their day. A stop at the Six Flags amusement park located about two hours from New York City had come in third on that visit. Unfortunately the day they visited the park had also been during opening weekend, and the lines had been longer than usual. The only upside had been at least it was a cool day so they hadn't melted while waiting for the rides.

Going through the obstacle course wasn't on his agenda today. Instead he envisioned them playing a round of mini golf at the best mini golf place he'd ever visited before taking out one of the swan boats for a relaxing trip around the lake. If Leah spotted the Above The Trees Adventure obstacle course and wanted to add it to the day, they could. Although he genuinely hoped it didn't appeal to Leah. In general he wasn't afraid of heights. He could ride the ski lift up to the top of any mountain and ski down without a second thought. The obstacle course was a different matter entirely. The idea of being more than ten feet in the air with nothing between him and the ground except a rope and a nylon harness made him break out in a cold sweat. But he'd suffered through the experience for Erin. If Leah asked, he'd suffer through it again for her.

By the time they reached their destination, Gavin had a nice list of future outings tucked away in his memory. And although she hadn't guessed his plan for today, her first theory before leaving his condo had been a baseball game, which was actually what he hoped to do tomorrow. Eventually she gave up and their conversation turned to the novel

Fatal Deception. She managed to surprise the hell out of him when she slipped up and mentioned her brother had written the book. He didn't know the guy well, but he couldn't picture Curt sitting at a computer for hours writing about fictional characters. Then again, Gavin had a hard time imagining Leah's brother remodeling houses, and he knew it had been Curt's hobby for some time.

"Essex Recreational Complex," Leah read aloud as they passed though the entrance. "I've never heard of it, but unless it's for work I don't visit New Jersey."

He navigated his way through parking lot A before finding a spot with some shade. It wouldn't prevent the car from warming up, but it would keep it a few degrees cooler than most of the other spots.

"What's on the agenda while we're here?" she asked.

"Anything you want. But I thought we could play a round of mini golf to start." He took her hand as they moved away from his car. "I've never visited a better mini golf facility than Paradise Fairway."

"Then you've never been to Pirate's Cove in Newport," Leah replied.

Gavin shook his head. He'd taken Erin to the popular mini golf park. While he agreed the place was nice and had excellent ice cream, the facility here topped it. "Pirate's Cove is okay, but this place is better."

"I'll be the judge of that."

"Just wait, you'll see. After, I thought we could rent one of the swan boats. But if you see anything else you want to try, say the word." He paused before a sign listing the various activities inside the complex and where to find them.

"I'm up for anything here except this." Leah pointed toward the listing for the Above The Trees Adventure. "Sounds like one of those obstacles courses where they expect you to walk on ropes and zip line from one platform to another. Between you and me, I am not a fan of heights. I think it's one of the reasons I don't like skiing. Riding those ski lifts always freaks me out."

They turned down the path leading to the mini golf course. "I've been though it once and have no desire to go again."

In his opinion, calling Paradise Fairway a mini golf course was doing the place a disservice. The facility actually consisted of three separate courses. The one labeled bronze was a basic nine-hole course with silly cartoonlike animals placed throughout it, and for the most part relatively easy shots. It was the perfect course for young children, especially those who got bored easily. A much longer eighteen-hole course labeled the silver course was his daughter's favorite and the one they went through most of the time. The shots tended to be more challenging yet not impossible. At the same time, the course contained those obstacles people expected to find on a mini golf course such as windmills and barn doors that opened and closed in an attempt to stop a player from getting the ball in the hole.

But his favorite here was the gold course. The twenty-four holes were spread out through a maze of trees and flowers. A small stream flowed past several of the holes and sometimes even though many of the greens. On countless occasions he'd had a ball land in the water. Sometimes he managed to fish it out before it washed away and other times he didn't. The facility kept small buckets of extra balls at many of the greens so if you lost one you didn't need to walk all the way back to the customer service booth for a new one.

A teenager with a bad case of acne looked up from his cell phone, a look of pure annoyance on his face when Gavin greeted him. "Bronze, silver, or gold?" he asked in a tone bordering on rude.

Policing someone else's employees wasn't his job, so he

refrained from suggesting the kid get a better attitude if he hoped to keep his job. "Two for the gold course," he replied, handing over his credit card.

The employee gave Gavin a scorecard as he ran the credit card. "The balls and clubs are behind you. Return them here when you're done." The teen handed him back his credit card and then started typing on his phone again.

When he played mini golf, he always used the dark blue ball. Erin always went for the bright yellow, and if Piper was with them, she picked the pink one. This afternoon when he reached for the blue one, his fingertips landed on it the same time as Leah's.

"If you want this one, I'll take another color," she said, moving her hand away.

He didn't much care what color he used. They all did the same job. "Doesn't matter to me, I just thought you'd go for the pink or purple one."

Leah selected a black one instead before removing a blue ball and handing it to him. "Dark blue and red are my favorite colors. They always have been. Purple is okay, but pink ranks down near the bottom unless we're talking about nail polish."

Gavin stored the detail away. A guy never knew when it might be useful to know his girlfriend's favorite color.

~

THEY MANAGED to make it through the whole course without losing a ball, a feat he couldn't remember happening in a long time. After, they both attempted the final extra shot of the course, an impossible shot that if anyone made earned them a gift card for three free visits. He'd brought Erin to the course numerous times and he'd never seen anyone make the shot.

Until today.

Like a pro, Leah hit the ball with just enough power to send it up the ramp and through the narrow opening, where it then landed in the hole instead of the gap surrounding it—which was where his ball ended up.

"I still cannot believe you made that last hole," he commented as they waited in line for ice cream. "Are you secretly a mini golf pro?"

In addition to making the impossible shot at the end, she'd successfully made all but two holes under par. According to the employee at the customer service booth, Leah's score was the second-best ever for the course and the employee added their scorecard to the Wall of Stars.

"Is that even a thing?"

They moved forward as the customers in front of them received their orders. "I don't think so, but who knows. People play video games for a living, why not mini golf too?"

Ice cream in hand, they headed out for a leisurely stroll along the walking path. Although parts of the path took them through wooded areas and around the lake, it also led them past the entrances to the antique carousel and to the Above The Trees Adventure. Today the place appeared packed as both adults and children made their way across ropes and down zip lines.

"Yeah, that's definitely not the place for me." Leah pointed at a woman as she zip-lined from one wooden platform to another.

"Erin couldn't get enough when we went through it. She's bugging me to come back when she comes and stays with me."

She raised her ice-cream cone to her lips, but rather than take a bite she said, "Between snowboarding, skiing, and that," Leah pointed toward the course, "she sounds like a bit of an adrenaline junkie."

Anyone who spent an hour with his daughter knew she

had the energy of two children her age. "She doesn't like to sit still, and she'll try anything once."

"Sounds like my brother Brett. There's nothing he won't do. He made more trips to the emergency room than all my cousins, Curt, and me combined. I think half my mom's gray hairs were caused by him."

His daughter might be adventurous, but at least she hadn't required any hospital visits because of it. At least not yet. Considering how active the girl was, it wouldn't shock him if she found herself there eventually. "So far the worst Erin's got was a bloody nose at soccer. Fingers crossed it stays that way."

The path rounded a corner leading them past the south entrance of the mini golf course before it again disappeared into the woods, providing them with some much-appreciated shade. His weather app still claimed it might rain tonight, but the sky said otherwise. There wasn't a cloud in sight. Unfortunately, it had been right about the record high temperature today. The high humidity level wasn't helping either.

"Time to be honest. Was I right?" He gestured over his shoulder in the general direction of Paradise Fairway.

Rather than answer immediately, she took a large bite from her ice cream. "Maybe," she admitted. "But Pirate's Cove has much better ice cream."

"You won't get any disagreement from me there, but if you want some incredible ice cream, you need to go to Ludlow Farm. It's in Pennsylvania. A Mennonite family owns it, and everything in the store is homemade. I don't think I've ever had ice cream anywhere that comes even close to what they make. I stop in whenever I'm in the area."

She popped the last of her cone in her mouth and licked off the ice cream still clinging to her thumb. "If the ice cream they make is better than Pirate's Cove, I need to plan a trip there. What do you say? Are you up for a little weekend getaway soon?"

With the exception of his once-a-year weekend trip to Maine, he didn't go on weekend gateways. Last Saturday and Sunday aside, when he traveled overnight, it was for one of two reasons: work or to see his daughter. But if Leah wanted to spend a weekend sampling every ice cream stand in and around Elizabethtown, Pennsylvania, he'd sample right along with her.

SEVEN

"Make yourself comfortable while I get started on the rest of my surprise," Gavin said, following her inside the condo.

Up to now, the day had proceeded with only a single interruption when he received a call from his mom. Although she lived in Rhode Island with her husband, Clark, they didn't get together as often as either would like. Instead they spoke about once a week or so. Today he kept his conversation as short as possible without being rude and then invited her and Clark to visit when Erin was with him at the end of the month.

He hoped the call was the first and only interruption. He intended to prepare them a meal to rival anything they'd get at their country club, and he didn't need work or family bothering him while he cooked.

"Rest? You've got me intrigued."

Stepping up behind her, Gavin wrapped his arms around her waist. "Good," he whispered against her neck before kissing her. "Make yourself at home while I start dinner."

She glanced over her shoulder at him. Her expression

echoed both curiosity and surprise. "As in cook a meal?" Leah turned in his arms.

"Yep." Her lips called out to him, but if he gave in to his desire now, he'd never want to stop, and his well-thought-out meal would never happen. After kissing her on the forehead instead, he took a step back. "If we want to eat at a decent time, I need to get started."

Leah followed him into the kitchen, and he could feel her eyes on him as he moved to the refrigerator and started taking out ingredients.

"I can handle the basics—pasta, scrambled eggs, grilled cheese sandwiches—but not much else. And it's not that I haven't tried. I even had Gray's wife give me a few lessons, but I can't seem to master it."

Cooking was one skill he'd mastered at a fairly young age thanks to his grandmother. "Some people have a knack for it."

She made herself comfortable on a barstool near the counter and asked, "You really know how to cook?"

Gavin left the steak tips and portobello mushrooms on the counter before returning to the refrigerator. "I don't do it as much as I'd like because I'm not home for meals. But my grandmother, Dad's mom, and I used to spend hours cooking together."

"I used to spend hours shopping with my grandmother. Even now we'll go when she comes to the city. I usually get tired and call it a day before she does," Leah admitted with a slight shake of her head. "I don't know how she does it, but I hope I'm half as energetic when I'm her age."

He added the butter, cream, and shallots he needed for the sauce to the ingredients already out. "Sounds like she'd get along well with my grandmother. Gigi's still a whirlwind in the kitchen."

"Anything I can help with?"

When he cooked, he preferred to work alone, especially if the person didn't have much of a clue in the kitchen, which Leah had already admitted she didn't. The only exception was Erin, but when they cooked together, the meals were far less elaborate.

Leaning over the counter between them, he kissed her. The awkward position kept him from lingering too long. Considering he wanted to enjoy dinner sometime this century, it was for the best. "All set, but I'd love your company."

"It's probably a better idea if I stay on this side of the kitchen anyway. You've got a lot of ingredients out; what are you making?"

Since she often ordered beef when they ate out, he assumed it ranked among her favorite type of meal. With this in mind, he'd focused mainly on beef dishes he excelled at before settling on the beef tips. "Steak tips with grilled portobello mushrooms in a brandy peppercorn cream sauce, along with au gratin potatoes and a salad."

She blinked several times. "Wow, you weren't joking when you said you knew how to cook." She sounded impressed. "That sounds like something Gray's wife would make."

Gavin would accept such a compliment any day, because he knew the woman Leah referred to was a professional chef at one of Rhode Island's best French restaurants—a restaurant he frequently visited when he was in Providence.

"Wait until you taste what I've got planned for dessert." Ice cream or no ice cream at the park, he planned to make his grandmother's signature dessert for Leah tonight.

In an effort to save time, he'd done some prep work this morning before eking out some time in his office. And before hitting the sack last night, he'd toasted the oats for the dessert and left them soaking in whiskey so they'd be ready. Unfortunately, some parts of the meal he couldn't start early. So while he prepared the cream sauce and then moved on from there, Leah filled him in on her visit with her cousin the previous evening.

"He's going to ask Paige to marry him soon," she said, stealing a cucumber slice off the cutting board.

Gavin grabbed a slice for himself before checking on the steak tips. "Your cousin told you that?" If and when he proposed, he wouldn't announce it to anyone beforehand—not even to his twin sister, and he told Vivian a lot.

She shook her head and reached for another cucumber. "Scott refused to answer me when I asked. But when I watch them together, I can just tell. They're perfect for each other, and they've been living together for a while."

At one time, he'd thought Amber was the one for him. They'd even shared an apartment for almost a year, but eventually the things they wanted in life came between them. Except for the information Leah had shared, he didn't know anything about her cousin's relationship. But he did know that until the guy bought a ring and proposed, anything could happen.

Rather than share his sentiments, he said, "Scott has a son, doesn't he?"

"Cooper turned—"

The sound of an old-fashioned telephone ringing cut Leah off.

"Can you see who the caller is?" He'd left the cell phone on the counter across the kitchen, and he didn't want to stop working unless necessary.

Vivian had left a message earlier in the week, wanting to know how things had gone over Fourth of July weekend. He'd never gotten around to calling her back. With Leah sitting across from him, he wasn't going to answer any of her questions now either. So if it was his twin, she could leave another message, and he'd call her when he got a chance. Harry didn't call often, but he occasionally reached out on the weekends. Gavin sure as hell didn't want to talk to him tonight.

Grabbing the phone, Leah checked the screen. "It's your dad." She returned with the device and held it toward him.

Unless indisposed, he rarely blew off calls from either of his parents. "I'll keep it short," he promised before answering the call.

DETERMINING whether the call from Gavin's dad pertained to work or family from his responses was impossible. Rather than speak in complete sentences, Gavin answered with a series of noes with a few yeses thrown in. She'd heard friends have more in-depth conversations with their pets. Never mind pets, she had more interesting conversations with herself sometimes.

"Say hi to Kerry and Piper. I'll see you on Monday." He ended the call and returned to the salad he'd started putting together.

Gavin didn't get calls from his dad often, or if he did, it was never when they were together. "Everything okay?"

He dried the green pepper he'd washed and then sliced it in half. "Dad wanted to know if I'd heard from Harry. They were supposed to play tennis this afternoon, but he never showed up."

As far as she was concerned, Harry Kincaid ranked just slightly above pond scum. Still, she hoped nothing had happened to him. Pond scum or not, he was Gavin's half brother. "Your dad's worried about him?"

They might all be adults, but if either she or one of her

brothers didn't show up when they were expected, both her parents would be concerned.

"Annoyed. Harry pulls this kind of stuff too often for Dad to worry." Gavin removed the seeds from inside the pepper before cutting it into cubes. "He's probably with his girlfriend and couldn't be bothered to call Dad. He doesn't have much consideration for anyone. He never has."

Once again she wondered why she'd stayed with Harry for as long as she had. Sure, he could be charming, but he had a lot of bad habits. Some of them he'd managed to keep hidden until near the end of their relationship. Others she'd picked up on right away, but she'd been willing to overlook them because she'd kept telling herself Tory, her cousin and best friend, wouldn't consider Harry a friend if he was a bad guy. It wasn't until after Leah ended the relationship that she learned Tory had introduced them because her fiancé and Harry were close friends. Correction, Tory's *former* fiancé; Luke and Tory had parted ways the previous month.

"Milan will get tired of him fast," she predicted.

A picture of the supermodel and Harry leaving a New York hotel had popped up on a popular internet site she visited. Although Leah wouldn't call the supermodel a close friend, they knew each other. But even if they didn't, Leah was familiar with the woman's reputation. Regardless of whether the man she was dating was a famous athlete or even an A-list actor, she never stayed with them for long.

"Had a similar thought when I saw they were together," Gavin responded. "And I don't care."

She watched him open a bottle of red wine before removing the potatoes from the oven. "Milan and her sister Brooklyn remind me of you and Harry."

He tossed a skeptical look her way as he took down two glasses. "I'm not sure I want to know how."

Leah might consider Milan a mere acquaintance, but

she'd known Brooklyn even before she became a Sherbrooke the previous year. "They have almost nothing in common and don't share much of a family resemblance. Just like you and Harry."

"Can't disagree with you there," he said. "The dining room will be more comfortable. If you bring in the wine, I'll take care of everything else."

Located at the rear of the condo, the dining room had windows stretching from the floor to the ceiling. While the room was tastefully furnished, it usually lacked any warmth or personality. This evening was a different story.

A small centerpiece of flowers occupied the middle of the table. White taper candles stood on either side of it. Napkins folded to resemble fans sat inches from the silverware.

Setting down the wine and the glasses, she moved to pull out the chair closest to her. She didn't get a chance to do anything else.

After setting two dinner plates on the table, Gavin's hands came down over hers and his chest brushed against her back. "Let me," he said, his voice a caress that did crazy things to her insides.

He might only be talking about pulling out her chair, but at the moment she was close to letting him do anything he wanted.

Once she sat, he pushed her chair in. Many considered it both an old-fashioned and unnecessary gesture, and she wouldn't want him to do it all the time, but it suited the moment.

"This looks and smells amazing. If it tastes even half as good as it smells, you went into the wrong line of work." And she wasn't telling him that because he'd gone to so much effort.

~

THE DESSERT before her looked so pretty she was reluctant to disturb it. However, it did contain raspberries, and they were one of her favorite fruits. The only fruit she enjoyed more was cherries. Dipping her spoon in, she scooped up a generous portion of the concoction he'd put together after dinner.

The taste of sweet raspberries, cream, honey, toasted oats, and something she recognized but couldn't label exploded in her mouth. "Where has this dessert been all my life?" she asked.

With a chuckle, Gavin started on his own portion. "Scotland."

"If Scotland has desserts like this, I need to spend more time there. What is it called?"

"Cranachan. It's one of my grandmother's favorite desserts."

She licked the last of the cream off her spoon before returning it to the glass for more. "She's the one who started the company?"

"No, Gigi's parents opened the first restaurant. They moved to the US right after World War I and named it Culloden after the village in Scotland where my great-grandmother came from. But Gigi's the one who expanded the business by buying other chains and then starting a few new ones."

"And she's the one who taught you to cook?"

He nodded. "Vivian too, and she does it a lot more than me. Gigi has started showing Piper and wants to get Erin in the kitchen. But it hasn't happened yet."

Leah took another bite of her dessert and again tried to identify the unique flavor she kept picking up. "What's in this besides the obvious?"

"Whiskey. The oats soaked in it overnight." He reached

for his coffee and added a generous amount of cream and sugar.

"You started preparing all this last night?"

He'd driven to and from Maine yesterday and still had taken the time to soak toasted oaks so he could make her dessert. She'd had some thoughtful boyfriends in the past, but he set the bar at a whole new level.

"It's not the same if you don't," he admitted. "There's some left in the kitchen if you want more."

She eyed what was left in her dessert glass. "I'm not sure I can finish this."

Leah hated to admit defeat, but tonight her only option was to retreat and leave behind a decent portion of her dessert. Even an hour after finishing their meal, she remained full, but thankfully not stuffed, while she relaxed and watched the light show Mother Nature was putting on outside.

Some people were afraid of thunder and lightning. She'd seen friends go deathly pale at the slightest rumble of thunder. Not her. She'd always loved storms like this. And if the wind picked up and the skies opened while one was going on, all the better. Even when they caused the power to go out, she enjoyed them. Tonight was no different. Wanting a better view, Leah left Gavin on the sofa talking to his daughter and crossed the room.

A bright flash streaked through the sky and a moment later a powerful boom rocked the silence, indicating the storm was closer. The sound of rain pelting glass soon followed, and Leah couldn't contain a slight smile. The weather gods had her in mind tonight.

Behind her the table lamps flickered twice before going out, but Mother Nature quickly lit up the room with its own light. From the sofa she heard Gavin tell his daughter he'd talk to her later.

"Something interesting out there?" Gavin asked, joining her.

"Just enjoying the show," she explained.

"You like this kind of weather?" He sounded skeptical.

"Love it. Before I knew how dangerous it could be, I would beg my mom to let me go outside and watch."

"I think you're the only person I know who likes storms."

She turned toward him. "Not all storms. Just ones like this. I hate when it snows, and rain showers are more of a nuisance. But this," she gestured at the window, "is different."

The lack of lights in the room cast his face in shadows, but she could tell he didn't share her opinion. Not many people did, and she was okay with that.

Placing his hands on her waist, Gavin pulled her closer. "Then the next time we have one, I'll let you watch and enjoy it." He lowered his head, but he stopped before his lips reached hers. "But not tonight."

Warm lips came down on hers. All the kisses they'd shared today had been sweet but much too short, in her opinion. Stretching up on to her tiptoes, she traced his bottom lip with her tongue. Gavin didn't require any further encouragement. He thrust his tongue inside her mouth and at the same time lifted her off her feet. When she wrapped her legs around his waist and felt his erection pressing into her, she groaned.

Thunder rumbled outside, mimicking the sound her heart was making inside her chest. And although she'd counseled herself the previous weekend that taking it slow was the best course, her body was demanding she follow a different path tonight.

With his hands cradling her butt and her legs wrapped around his waist, she was confident she wouldn't fall if she removed her arms from around his neck. She ended their kiss and pulled back. Immediately disappointment flickered in Gavin's eyes. When she reached for the hem of her top, it disappeared just as quickly. Heat hot enough to singe her hair replaced it.

His eyes followed her hands as she inched the material higher and over her head. Then she dropped the top on the floor before unclasping her bra and slipping it off. All her adult life, she'd considered her breasts too small. More than once she'd thought of having them enlarged a cup size or two. The idea of undergoing surgery and then recovery always stopped her.

The way Gavin was staring at her breasts now made her wonder if she'd been too critical of them all these years.

Gavin slammed his lips down on hers again and started walking. Instinctively she put her arms around his shoulders again, causing his T-shirt to rub against her sensitive nipples, and tried to move against his erection. The hands on her backside made it impossible. He didn't move his hands when he sat on the sofa, forcing her to straddle his lap. Pressed so intimately against him, she couldn't stop her body from moving. Intense pleasure shot through her, and all she could think about was doing it again.

The hand now on her waist stopped her and held her in place. Moving his lips away from hers, he took one breast in his hand as he lowered his head. Slowly he flicked his thumb back and forth against her nipple. Then when she thought it couldn't get any tighter, he blew on it. The warm breath sent tingles across her breast and she shivered. Finally he touched it with the tip of his tongue before closing his lips around it.

Groaning, she reached for his hand still on her waist. He didn't resist when she pulled it away and moved it to her other breast. While his lips and tongue teased one nipple, his hand caressed the other.

With both his hands occupied, there was nothing to stop

Leah from moving against him the way her body was urging her to.

He released her nipple and looked up at her. "I want to take my time tonight. If you don't stop doing that, I'm not going to be able to."

The fire reflected in his eyes only fueled the flames licking her body. Reaching between them, she unbuttoned his shorts and slipped her hand inside. Gently she stroked him, his skin hot against her palm.

She couldn't remember ever wanting a man as much as she wanted Gavin now. "We can go slow next time."

SOMETIME BETWEEN THE first and second time they made love, the thunder and lightning stopped. Since then the rain had also ended, and the sky had cleared. Now, moonlight filled the room, allowing him to see the naked woman in bed next to him.

Turning on his side, Gavin propped himself up on an elbow. "Stay here tonight." He ran a hand across her stomach and then down her thigh. "I'll make you breakfast in the morning."

"Tempting offer," she replied, placing her hand over his and holding it in place on her thigh.

"But?" he asked when Leah didn't give him a more satisfactory answer.

She pulled his hand along her leg and up to her waist. "How do your breakfasts compare to your dinners?"

"Almost as good," he admitted, reaching for the sheet when Leah shivered. "And if you stay, I promise you more than a good meal." Under the sheet, he cupped her breast and flicked this thumb against her nipple.

"Your offer is sounding better and better." Moving onto

her side, she swung one leg over his. "Before I accept, I need another demonstration of what I can expect in the morning." Leah took his hand and moved it down her body and between her legs.

He'd given her two such demonstrations already. If she wanted another, he was more than happy to oblige.

EIGHT

Gavin glanced at his watch. This meeting with his father had started almost two hours ago, and he needed to wrap it up so he could focus on other issues requiring his attention—issues he wanted to tackle before he left the office for the weekend, because he didn't want to take work home with him. Unfortunately, Dad didn't seem to be in any rush this afternoon, because although they'd covered everything on the agenda, he still sat at the conference table in Gavin's office.

"This evening I'm meeting Fredrick at the club for a round of golf. Why don't you join us," he suggested. "We can have dinner while we're there. Kerry and Piper are away visiting Kerry's mom for the weekend."

Occasionally he spent time with Dad outside the office. The man was a good golf player, and Gavin always had to play his best if wanted to beat him. The same was true of Dad's longtime friend Fredrick Wayland. Perhaps four or five months ago he would've accepted the invitation, but ever since Harry had shared their father's request regarding Leah, he'd avoided Dad as much as possible. Yes, in the long run Dad's insistence that Harry stay with Leah hadn't caused her any permanent damage, but he never should've proposed the idea, and Gavin couldn't forgive him for doing it.

He closed the open laptop on the table and stacked his legal pad on top. "I can't. I have plans tonight," Gavin answered. At the moment, he and Leah had no specific plans other than to spend time with each other, but Dad didn't need to know that.

"Maybe next time then," Dad replied.

His father stood and Gavin sent up a silent thank-you.

"If you change your mind, Fredrick and I are meeting at five o'clock. Fredrick's daughter, Laurel, will be there as well. I was hoping to introduce you to her."

Gavin had known Fredrick much of his life, but he'd never met his only daughter. From all accounts the woman was and always had been a high-maintenance spoiled princess.

"Isn't she married?" The only reason he remembered the woman had gotten married was because Piper had been her flower girl. She'd talked about little else for months leading up to the ceremony three or so years ago.

Dad shook his head and sat back down again.

Me and my big mouth.

"Her divorce from Blake Goldman was finalized back in the winter, and she just moved back to the city. I think the two of you would get along well together."

Never in his life had Dad showed any interest in his love life. If he was doing so now, it wasn't because Dad wanted him to be happy. No, he had a specific reason, and Gavin had no interest in knowing what it was.

"Set her up with Harry. I'm not interested."

"After the way he blew things with the Sherbrooke woman? Not a chance."

Before he heard any more and had even more reason to dislike his father, he needed to nip this one in the ass. "I'm with someone." And he needed to get back to work so he could focus on her for the next two days. "If you'll excuse me, I have a few things to finish up before I call it a night."

Dad didn't argue, but the muscle twitching in his jaw told Gavin everything he needed to know. "Have a nice weekend," he offered up before he exited the office.

I plan to.

Gavin carried his laptop and legal pad back to his desk. Opening the device, he got ready to get back to work. The ringing coming from his pants pocket stopped him.

Immediately he assumed the call was from Erin. Leah never called him during the day. Instead she sent him a text message, and if she needed to talk, she'd ask him to call when he had a moment. Vivian rarely called him before eight o'clock, his time.

Pulling the device out, he checked the screen. Instant dread shot through him when he saw Leah's name displayed there.

"Are you okay?" he asked in lieu of a proper greeting, because if she was calling at three in the afternoon, something must be wrong.

"Of course," she assured him. "I just need to know what's the earliest you think you can get home tonight."

He ran through his mental to-do list. He had enough to keep him here well past dinnertime. "Why?"

"I have something special planned, and I need to have an approximate time."

Curiosity piqued, he replied, "Does six work?"

"Yep, thank you."

"Do I get any hints about what you have in store for me?" Over breakfast they'd talked about playing it by ear this weekend rather than making any specific plans.

"Nope. I'll see you in a little while."

LEAH ENDED the conversation and dialed her cousin's flight crew so they knew approximately when to expect her and Gavin this evening. With their travel plans settled, she turned back to the open document on her computer.

As the global chief communications and public affairs officer for the company, one of her many responsibilities was to oversee Sherbrooke Enterprises' philanthropic efforts. One project they were considering getting involved with was Anderson Brady's Clean Water Matters project. Although her meeting with Anderson had been promising, before she moved ahead she needed to review the large amount of information he'd presented her with. Since the meeting was still fresh in her mind, she'd start wading her way through it before she left.

The office door opened and Diane, her personal assistant, stuck her head inside. "Mr. Talbot is here to see you. Are you available?" she asked.

"Please send him in."

Dylan Talbot, the current CEO of Sherbrooke Enterprises, entered her office, closing the door behind him. Although not related except through marriage, she'd known Dylan her entire her life and thought of him as more a cousin than a mere friend and coworker.

"How was your meeting with Anderson?" he asked in his oh-so-lovely British accent. Regardless of how she viewed him or the fact he was married to her cousin, she would happily sit around any day of the week and listen to him speak, even if it was to deliver a weather report.

"Good. He's done far more with the project than I realized."

When she first learned of the actor's project, she assumed it was some kind of publicity stunt, that once Anderson milked the project for all it was worth, he'd dismiss it and move on to something else. Rather than dismissing it, he'd expanded the charity and helped bring clean drinking water to people who needed it most.

"He left me with a lot of data to go through."

"Gray's only had good things to say about the project," Dylan replied. He sat in one of the two chairs near her desk and moved the large vase of flowers Gavin had sent her off to one side so they could have a conversation without it between them.

Dylan made sure he kept well informed about as many aspects of the company as humanly possible. "I can pass this data on to you once I'm finished," she offered.

"No need. I didn't actually come down to talk to you about Anderson. I wanted to let you know Callie's going to invite you to dinner tonight. Dad and Pauline are here," he explained.

Prior to the birth of Dylan's son, she'd only met Dylan's father and stepmother, who lived in England, once, and it had been at Dylan and Callie's wedding. Since the birth of his first grandson, she'd seen Dylan's father and his wife countless times at Callie and Dylan's home. And although not people she'd call if she wanted to hang out for an evening—they were a little uptight—she liked them both.

"Before she does and you say yes, I feel it's only fair I warn you Callie has an ulterior motive. Chase will be there too. He arrived last night," Dylan continued.

Dylan's younger half brother lived in England too, and much like their father, he'd rarely made the trip across the Atlantic before the birth of James, Dylan's son. Now Chase made regular visits to Dylan and Callie's home. At one point Callie had mentioned that he was thinking about buying a home in the area. Since he still crashed at Dylan and Callie's when he came, he'd either not found the right one or he'd changed his mind.

"Callie wants to get the two of you together," he finished.

"When did she start playing Cupid?"

"You're her first victim," Dylan admitted.

"Lucky me."

They hadn't talked since before the party in Newport, and since Callie and Dylan hadn't attended the bash that weekend, Callie didn't know Leah was no longer single.

"But she'll have to use her love arrows on someone else. Maybe Juliette." Having only met Chase a handful of time, she didn't know him well, but she got the impression he wouldn't be a good match for her cousin Courtney, which left Courtney's sister as the only remaining possibility. "I'm with someone," she explained.

"Bring him with you. Callie won't mind."

"We're heading to Martha's Vineyard this weekend."

After suggesting they should visit the island back on the Fourth while talking to Tasha, she'd dismissed all thought of the place from her mind. It hadn't returned until yesterday. Gavin had put a lot of thought and effort into making the previous weekend special, and she wanted to reciprocate. Whisking him off to Martha's Vineyard for a few days fit the bill.

A quick call to Sara before her meeting with Anderson had taken care of their lodging needs. A second call to Scott had taken care of their transportation needs, leaving her with nothing else to do except pack.

"Have fun." Dylan stood. "I'll see you next week."

For the remainder of the afternoon, she found her thoughts continually veering off what she should be doing and to what she would be doing once they arrived at Sara's house. Spending time with Gavin, regardless of whether they were lounging on the sofa or naked in his bed, was always delightful. She never felt the need to act, think, or even dress a certain way. With him she could be herself. Until their relationship, she hadn't realized how much of herself she held back with other men. For the first time in her life, a man was seeing the true Leah Sherbrooke.

WHEN SHE WALKED in the door and told him to pack, he did as she'd asked without demanding additional details. When she drove them to the nearby state airport and escorted him onto the awaiting Gulfstream jet, he'd only asked whom it belonged to because he knew it wasn't hers.

But as the wheels touched down and the plane rolled to a stop, he couldn't keep from asking where they were. They'd been in the air for less than an hour, so it limited the possible destinations.

"Are you going to tell me where we are now?" he asked, moving his lips away from hers again. They'd spent a fair amount of the trip enjoying each other's company as much as possible without actually stripping each other's clothes off, making this by far the most enjoyable flight he'd ever had.

She ran the hand still under his shirt down his chest and across his abdomen, causing his muscles to contract. "Nope." With a wicked smile, she removed her hands from his body and reached for the purse she'd tossed on a nearby seat. "I need you to put this on." She held up a blue-and-white bandana.

He accepted the material and started tying it around the lower part of his face. "We're holding up a bank? Can I drive the getaway car?"

"Very funny." Leah untied the knot behind his head and moved the bandana up over his eyes. "I better not see you remove this until I tell you to."

Whatever she had planned, she'd thought it out. And while he was dying to know where they were, he'd play along tonight. "Just don't let me trip walking down any stairs."

"Don't worry, I won't let anything happen to you," she promised, taking his hand and leading him off the plane.

Gavin learned one thing on the car ride from the airport to their final destination: he didn't like being blindfolded, at least not in a car that was moving. Thankfully the ride was short, and in no time Leah was telling him to sit tight until she came around to the passenger side of the car.

The smell of the ocean and crashing waves gave him his first good clue of the evening.

"You have one step here," she told him before she released his hand.

He heard a series of short beeps, and he guessed she was putting in a code to unlock a door.

She slipped her hand into his again and they moved forward, the sound of the ocean disappearing.

"Did you have enough time to get everything done?" Leah stopped and spoke to someone.

"I came by and set everything up earlier, so it didn't take me long to finish once I received your text."

"Excellent. Thank you."

"Would you like me to return in the morning to prepare breakfast?"

"No, we'll be fine. Enjoy the rest of your night," Leah replied.

Whoever she'd enlisted to help walked away, their footsteps gradually receding.

What are you up to? If Leah had sent any text messages, she'd done it after blindfolding him.

"You only need to leave the blindfold on for a little longer," she said, resuming their trip.

Fresh air again washed over his face, and Gavin took in a deep breath of ocean air. "I need to spend more time at the beach," he said.

"We'll work on it. For now, have a seat and I'll be right back. Do. Not. Peek."

Yeah, right. "Whatever you say."

He waited until he could no longer hear her footsteps and reached for the material covering his eyes. She'd left him in an outdoor living room. To the left of him stood a large fireplace. At the moment it was empty, but on a cool evening it would be just the thing to keep the home's owners comfortable. The sofas were arranged in such a way that regardless of where you sat, you'd get a great view of the ocean, and fans hung from the ceiling. A bottle of wine sat chilling on the end table closest to where she'd left him, and whoever left the wine had also lit candles.

Before she came back and caught him, Gavin pulled the blindfold back down, because under no circumstances did he want to ruin whatever surprise she had planned.

He just lowered his hands back to his lap when she said, "I hope you didn't peek."

"Of course not." Gavin tried to reach for her, but she pushed his hands away. Reaching behind him, she untied the material over his eyes and let it drop to the ground.

And he almost followed.

The barely there lingerie she'd changed into revealed far more than it covered. She'd taken the braid out of her hair and left it loose around her shoulders. The slight breeze coming off the water made the flames on the candles dance, casting light across her sun-kissed skin.

Leah straddled his lap and smiled. "Welcome to Martha's Vineyard. I hope you enjoy the visit." She didn't give him a chance to reply.

NINE

They hadn't spent a weekend apart since the Fourth. In fact, since the evening he cooked Leah dinner almost two weeks ago, they'd only spent three nights apart. Most of the time she went to his place, but occasionally Gavin drove to her home in Connecticut after work instead. That had been the case last night, and when he left Leah's house this morning, she woke up long enough to ask him to call her once he got settled at his hotel.

Traveling around the country for work had never bothered him too much unless it interfered with seeing his daughter. All week though, he'd dreaded this trip. Unfortunately, there hadn't been any way around it. The only upside to the trip was he'd get a chance to see his sister. Vivian had invited him to stay with her rather than at a hotel, and while he appreciated the offer and would've normally accepted, he knew he'd get more done if he was able to return to an empty room each night, and he needed to make sure he stayed on top of all his projects while away.

In another week, Erin would be with him, and he intended to spend very little time worrying about anything other than enjoying their time together. Which was why, after checking into his hotel a few hours ago, he'd called Leah and then got right down to work. But with everything prepared for his meeting tomorrow, he could call it a day. He hadn't seen his twin sister in months, and he planned to spend the rest of the evening with her.

"I'm glad you're here," Vivian said, giving him a hug before he managed to enter the house. "I've missed you."

He returned the embrace and kissed her cheek before stepping inside and closing the door. "I've missed you too."

Vivian had lived on the opposite coast for years, so he should be used to her being so far away. He wasn't. In fact, he wished Harry were the one who'd moved to California instead of her.

"When did you do this?" He gestured toward her hair.

People often joked Vivian was an attractive female version of him. He had to agree. They'd both inherited their dad's dark hair and eyes, although Vivian's hair contained subtle red highlights that had been passed along by someone on their family tree. And while no one would ever call either of them short, they were both several inches shorter than their father, who was almost six foot six, and Harry. Today though, her dark hair was several shades lighter and much shorter than the last time he'd seen her.

"Back in June. I wanted a change," she explained. "You hate it." It wasn't a question but rather a statement.

When it came to his sister's fashion or hairstyle choices, of which she'd made some questionable ones in the past, he went with the old adage "if you don't have anything nice to say, don't say anything at all." "You're saying that, not me, Viv."

"You might not be saying it with words, but I can tell what you're thinking." She shrugged. "I'm not crazy about it either. The color and style looked much better in the magazine than they do on me. But it's only hair. It'll grow back, so I'm not stuck with it forever."

She studied him for a moment before she spoke again. "You look different. Happier or something."

The reflection greeting him every morning in the mirror looked the same to him. If it could somehow reflect how he felt on the inside, the man in the mirror would look much different than the one who'd been there a few months ago.

"I ordered some pizzas as soon as I got home. They should be here soon." She put an arm over his shoulder and started walking toward the kitchen. "And since I love you so much and I know you never get around to making it, I got everything ready so we can have Cranachan for dessert."

"I appreciate the effort, but you're wrong. I made it the weekend before last, along with a meal Gigi would approve of."

Vivian stepped through the French doors and onto the deck. A pitcher of what looked like iced tea was on the table along with two glasses. She reached for the glass already filled. "Sounds like we've got a lot of catching up do to." She took a sip from her drink before continuing. "And just so you know, I'm not letting you leave tonight until you tell me everything. And I really mean everything, Gavin."

When they'd spoken the previous week, he'd been driving to Connecticut, so their conversation had remained on the short side. Although he'd answered Vivian's questions about his time in Newport with Leah, he hadn't provided any additional details. Since they'd been on the phone, it'd been easy to keep the specifics to himself. Now that they were face-to-face, keeping anything from Vivian would be impossible. If they were in the same room, she always knew when he was either withholding information or lying. It was a trait he shared as well. Growing up, Vivian hadn't been able to keep anything from him either.

"Fourth of July must have been more than okay and fun if you're cooking her dinner, Gavin." She filled the other glass with tea and handed it to him. "Yes, those were your exact words when I asked how the weekend went."

"Who said I cooked dinner for anyone? I do have to eat too. Maybe I made the meal for myself."

"Sure, it's possible. It's also possible Harry will wake up tomorrow and decide to stop sleeping around and become a monk." She gestured for him to sit before pulling out a chair and sitting down.

"Scientists finding little green men living on Mars is more likely than Harry giving up woman."

She nodded in agreement. "True. But I still don't believe you cooked something that would impress Gigi just for yourself. So please start at the beginning and don't leave anything out this time."

If she wanted him to start at the beginning, then he'd start at the beginning. "I told you she invited me to the party. But it was more of a friendly demand than an invitation." He smiled at the memory of her outrage when he'd told her he planned to work on the Fourth. "She threatened to drag me out of my office if I didn't come willingly. She even insisted we drive down together because she was afraid I'd back out at the last minute."

"I'm liking her a lot already," Vivian commented.

As far as he knew, his sister had only met Leah once, and it had been a brief encounter. If their relationship continued the way he hoped, he wanted the two women to get to know each other better. Getting that to happen would be tricky, considering the distance between them, but he'd figure out the logistics of it later.

Gavin went back to giving his sister enough details to satisfy her curiosity without recounting the entire weekend. Or at least he tried. Vivian wasn't known for remaining quiet during a conversation, and several times she interrupted him to ask a question or make a comment.

"I still can't believe Tasha Marshall was hitting on you. Didn't she know you came with Leah?" Vivian asked, coming back outside carrying the pizzas that had just arrived and two plates.

"Beats me," he admitted. He hadn't thought about it one way or the other. "You know her?" Before the party, he'd never seen or heard of the woman.

"Mostly from fundraisers. Last time I saw her was about a year ago at the Helping Hands Bachelor auction. She made a complete fool of herself."

Gavin didn't wait for his sister. He opened the top pizza box and pulled out a slice. "I knew Mom went. I didn't know you did too."

She slid a plate his way before opening the second box. "It was for a good cause and I was in the area. I didn't bid on anyone, but it was an entertaining night. If they hold another one, I might go again."

Entertaining for her maybe, but it sounded like torture for the men to him. No matter how good of a cause, he wouldn't have participated in such an event even if someone threatened him with bodily harm.

Vivian added two slices of pizza to her plate but didn't start on either of them. Instead she grabbed a napkin and said, "If you want, I'll tell you all about it sometime."

His twin traveled a fair amount and enjoyed trying new things, so she usually had a lot of interesting stories to share. Her experience at a bachelor auction wasn't one he cared to hear about. "I'll pass, thanks."

With a shrug Vivian moved their conversation back on track. "A party at her parents' and a cookout at her brother's. Sounds like a busy weekend. Before you continue, did you tell her about Erin?"

He'd skipped over the conversation they'd had during the fireworks. He wasn't going to rehash it now either. "She knows all about Erin."

"Good. Please continue. I promise not to interrupt again."

Yeah, right.

When it came to her sex life, his twin had always been open with him, even when he didn't care to know, like when her first sexual experience had been with his then good friend in high school. He'd never shared her willingness to talk about what did or didn't happen in his bedroom. So while they enjoyed their pizza, he gave Vivian the condensed, G-rated version of the past few weeks. And even if his twin wanted to know all the intimate details, she knew not to ask if he'd slept with Leah.

"How does Harry feel about you dating his ex?" Until now she'd kept her promise and hadn't said a word.

"I don't think he knows." Other than at work, they hadn't spoken in weeks. He saw no need to tell Harry or anyone else whom he was involved with anyway. "If he doesn't like it when he finds out, that's his problem." Harry had had his chance with Leah and blown it.

"Is he still with Milan or has she realized what a jerk he is and moved on?"

"Beats me."

Vivian looked about to say something else when the sound of the doorbell reached them from inside. "I'm not expecting anyone but you tonight." She pushed back her chair and stood. "Be right back. It is probably another campaigner hoping to get my vote. They've already started coming around, and the primary isn't until September."

With his sister gone for the moment, he pulled out his cell and sent Leah a short text message. He'd prefer to call, but he didn't want to be in the middle of a conversation when Vivian returned. Almost immediately a reply appeared on the screen.

Call me when you get a chance, Gavin. I miss you.

Miss you too. Talk to you soon.

Gavin returned the device to his pocket as a male voice drifted outside. "I didn't think you'd mind if I stopped over."

So much for Vivian's theory about a campaigner at the door.

Interest piqued, he listened for his sister's reply. "I don't. I'm just surprised. I didn't think I'd see you until tomorrow."

It sounded like Vivian had been so busy prying into his personal life, she'd neglected to share some new developments in hers. That wasn't something she usually did, and he intended to give her a hard time about it later.

Vivian stepped back outside, her arm around a man he recognized but had never met. "Jeff, I'd like you to meet my brother Gavin." She swung her gaze toward him. "Gavin, this is—"

"Jeffrey Moore," he said. He'd watched the professional soccer player enough times to know exactly whom his sister had her arm around. Gavin shot Vivian a quick look to let her know she had some questions to answer later before extending his hand toward Jeffrey. "Nice to meet you."

A DRIVE UP to New Hampshire today hadn't been anywhere on her radar until last night. With Gavin in California until Sunday, she wanted something to occupy her free time. A visit up to see her brother and his newest project struck her as the perfect distraction, which was why she'd worked a half day from home before jumping on the highway and heading to New England. While with Curt, she intended to not only pass the time but also get some advice.

When she'd first found out Gavin had a daughter, it seemed like no big deal. She liked children and even assumed someday she'd have her own. The closer it got to Erin's arrival in New York, the more anxious she got. From what she'd seen, Curt's relationship with his girlfriend's niece was going well, so he was obviously doing something right. Hopefully he'd share some insight on how to develop a similar relationship with Gavin's daughter.

Following the GPS directions, she turned onto Marsh Road and passed the village green. At the moment, a small farmers' market was set up on it, but a sign near the entrance mentioned a car show would be held there tomorrow. When Curt first told her about the town, he'd referred to it as quaint. From the little she'd seen so far, Leah agreed with his assessment.

She'd only visited the first home Curt renovated. It'd been a cute cottage in upstate New York. She'd seen pictures of the other two, however, and the house she'd just parked in front of was by far the largest he'd tackled. Instantly she wondered if perhaps this time he'd undertaken more than he could handle.

It took a few minutes for her brother to answer the door. When he finally did, he wasn't alone. Reese stood next to him. Both wore clothes that had seen better days and old sneakers. Several paint smears were on Curt's arms, and Reese had one on her chin and a smaller one on her forehead.

"I didn't expect you for at least another hour," he greeted, releasing the door and taking a step back so she could enter.

"Except for a little around Hartford and then again around Worcester, I didn't hit any traffic today," Leah explained. Avoiding traffic had been the main reason she left the city when she did. The summer traffic heading northeast on a Friday could be horrendous.

"I'd hug you, but Reese and I have been painting."

"Yeah, your blue skin kind of gave you away. And since

you have more on you than Reese does, I'm guessing she's better at it than you."

The comment elicited a giggle from Reese, but Curt ignored it and closed the front door. "Feel free to explore while we clean up. It won't take us long."

Reese and Curt headed up the curved staircase, leaving her alone in the large wood-paneled foyer. Although smaller, it reminded her of the one inside her grandparents' home. Tipping her head back, she studied the mural covering the vaulted ceiling. Even faded it was beautiful, and she wondered if her brother intended to paint over it or have it restored. Her favorite part of the foyer, though, was the stained glass windows. A large one filled the space above the front door, allowing in sunlight, and two matching panels flanked the door.

She didn't know the house's history, but by the looks of the foyer, whoever built the home had had excellent taste. Anxious to see more, she walked down one of the two hallways. A few of the rooms she peeked in looked untouched while others had obviously been painted. The huge room at the back of the house was clearly a work in progress. Sheets of plastic covered the floor, and cans of paint sat in the middle of the room next to some rollers. Since the walls in the room were burgundy and not blue, Curt and Reese had been working somewhere else today.

"What do you think?"

At the sound of Curt's voice, she turned. "I'm glad you're the one doing all this work and not me," she replied. Painting her nails was about the only painting she engaged in. "Where's your sidekick?"

"After I helped her get the paint off, Reese went to change into a bathing suit."

"Are you finished in here or just getting started?" The room looked nice and she honestly couldn't tell.

"It's about half done. It's needs another coat, and I plan to replace the floor."

"Was this a dining room or something?" She crossed to the wall of French doors and looked out at the large veranda. At the moment it was empty, but she could picture it filled with various flowering plants and a few tables, or maybe a couple of benches.

"Ballroom. When I moved in mirrors were mounted on the walls and a mural similar to the one in the foyer covered the ceiling."

Cliff House in Newport had a ballroom, but considering the time period it had been built in it had never seemed odd to her. In the late nineteenth century, Newport had been the place to be. Pelham, New Hampshire, didn't seem like the place to be no matter the century.

"Why would anyone in this town need a ballroom?" Leah opened a door and stepped outside for a moment to get a better look at the backyard. Curt followed her out.

"The family who built the house were the wealthiest people in southern New Hampshire at the time, and they liked to entertain. Did you see the kitchen? I finished it last week."

"Not yet."

He took her hand and led her back inside. "Follow me." Other than when he discussed his writing, he'd never sounded as excited as he did now.

Reese nearly knocked them over as she rushed down the hall. "Curt, I'm ready to go swimming," she announced with an amount of excitement only a child could conjure up.

"I need to show my sister the kitchen before we head out back, short stuff."

Reese didn't complain but her smile dimmed as she turned and down the hallway, the sound of her flip-flops echoing around them.

Entering the kitchen, Leah came to an abrupt stop. If Curt

had done all this, he'd learned a lot since he first started this hobby of his. "You did all this by yourself?"

"Thanks for the vote of confidence," he replied, sounding a little hurt.

"Sorry, it's gorgeous. I didn't realize you were so good at this renovation stuff." She moved farther into the room to get a better look around. "It resembles Trent and Addie's kitchen."

"That was the idea." He moved past her and to the refrigerator. "Do either of you want something to drink?"

Reese didn't hesitate to answer. "Juice please."

Curt pulled out a juice box and a can of root beer for himself.

She didn't drink soda often and never kept it at home, but she loved both root beer and cream soda. "I'll have a root beer too."

"Can we go outside now?" Reese asked, already on her way to the side door.

Her brother handed her the soda and grabbed the bag of pretzels on the counter. "We're right behind you."

Neither of them had a chance to sit before Reese jumped into the pool.

"I think she's part fish," Curt said, opening the umbrella at one of the patio tables outside.

Leah watched the girl swim to the ladder, climb out, and head back toward the diving board. Once there, Reese cannonballed into the pool again.

"Don't take this the wrong way or anything, but does she spend every day with you?" she asked.

He popped open his soda and took a long swallow before answering. "Only Tuesdays and Fridays. Camp ends at three, and I pick her up because both Taylor and Priscilla are still at work. The rest of the week Priscilla gets out in time to get her."

"Curt, watch this," Reese called out before doing a handstand in the shallow part of the pool.

When Reese popped back up, Curt gave the girl two thumbs up. "Nice job."

"I never knew you had such a paternal streak." Unless holding a baby counted, until this summer she'd never seen him interact with any children. Yet he looked perfectly comfortable and at ease alone with Reese. "She really likes you. How did you win her over?"

"Promised to teach her to play lacrosse, and I let her teach me all she knows about soccer. I think I've played more soccer games in Taylor's backyard than I ever did in school." Curt shifted his gaze her way. "Things not going well with Gavin's daughter?"

"She's been in Florida all month with her mom, so I haven't met her. Gavin's picking Erin up next Friday and bringing her back to New York for two weeks. And honestly, I'm getting nervous."

"Why? You've been around kids before, Leah." He tore open the pretzel bag and pulled out a handful before sliding the bag her way.

"But all of them are still in diapers. It's easy to make them happy. Erin's nine." She estimated Reese was a little younger than nine, but not much. Whatever strategies he'd used with Reese in the beginning might also help her. "Since teaching Erin lacrosse is out, do you have any other suggestions?"

Rather than answer, he looked back at the pool where Reese was now floating around on a large pizza-shaped raft. "Reese was friendly from the beginning. The first time I had dinner at the house, she asked if I had a girlfriend. When I told her no, she suggested Taylor could be my girlfriend."

"You're not helping," Leah grumbled before pulling out several pretzels.

"Be yourself. Find something you both like and do it together," Curt suggested.

She'd hoped for something more enlightening, but it was a start. Once Gavin had started talking about Erin, she'd learned the girl loved all kinds of physical activity and art. There was no shortage of art museums in and around the city, and Leah could happily spend hours at any of them. A day exploring one might be the perfect way to start building a relationship with Erin. When Gavin returned on Sunday, she'd run the idea by him.

Leah watched the girl relaxing in the pool. "Did she really say Taylor should be your girlfriend in the middle of dinner?"

Her brother picked up his soda can again. "It was at the end of dinner, but yeah. First she wanted to know if I had kids. Then she asked about a girlfriend. When I said no, she made her recommendation and added in how her grandmother was always telling Taylor to date more."

She envisioned the scene in her head and laughed. "Just a little embarrassing for everyone."

"I don't know about all children, but Reese says anything that comes into her head. If Gavin's daughter is anything like her, be prepared for some entertaining conversations while she's around," he warned.

They both remained silent and enjoyed the sun while Reese swam. Eventually another concern that had been popping up over the past week had Leah looking over at her brother. She'd never dated a man with a child, so she had no idea what kind of changes to expect when Erin came to New York. Would Gavin prefer she not stay at his place while his daughter was around? Two weeks without sex certainly wouldn't kill either of them, but she'd miss it. Even more, she'd miss falling asleep and waking up next to him, if he decided it was better she not spend the nights with him.

Although Reese was not biologically her daughter, Taylor

was, in all the ways that mattered, Reese's mom. How did her brother and Taylor handle the more intimate side of their relationship?

"I'm not looking for details or anything, but how do you and Taylor handle sex?" she asked, her voice much lower than normal even though she doubted Reese could hear them on her raft in the pool.

Curt's hand paused inside the pretzel bag. "The same way everyone does. Didn't Mom have the birds and bees talk with you?" he asked with a grin.

"Very funny. You know that's not what I meant." She yanked the bag away from him and pulled out a handful for herself. "Reese and Taylor stayed with you in Newport. Did Taylor sleep with you or did she stay in a separate room? And I'm sure you don't go weeks without sex, so either Taylor comes here or you go to her house."

Her brother's grin disappeared and his expression grew serious. "When we're in Newport we share a room, but Taylor gets up before Reese so she doesn't know we sleep in the same bed. Priscilla has no problem staying with Reese, so we get plenty of time alone, but Taylor never stays the night here." He touched her arm. "You're going to have to talk to Gavin about this one."

TEN

Some time with her brother, or more specifically, Reese, eliminated most of Leah's anxiety about meeting Erin later in the week. Throughout the weekend, Reese was just as outgoing and friendly to her as she was to Curt. When Taylor's mom invited them over for a cookout Saturday afternoon, Reese pulled Leah into the soccer game she, Curt, and Taylor were having before they ate. Later, she insisted Leah had to come upstairs and see her stuffed animal collection. And the girl had quite the collection. Leah was positive the assortment of furry friends surpassed the one she'd had as a child.

And Curt was right. The girl really did seem to say everything that came into her head, including telling everyone about how her best friend, Hazel, was about to have a new stepdad and baby brother, two bits of information that for some reason had left both Taylor and Priscilla speechless.

Despite enjoying her time in New Hampshire, she'd left her brother's after breakfast. With Gavin due back that evening, she returned to her place in the city instead of Greenwich so he wouldn't have a long drive after a full day of travel. As she'd expected when she shared her intention, he told her not to worry about it. He knew she preferred her house in Connecticut to the apartment. But she'd held firm and promised to be there when he arrived.

After dropping her overnight bag in the bedroom, Leah switched on her favorite country playlist. Until recently country had been one of the few styles she didn't listen to. Her cousin's wife, Addie, had introduced Leah to songs by some of her favorite bands though, and ever since she'd been adding more and more country to her music collection. Somehow over the past year, the number of country songs she owned had doubled. Now she had more of them than she did classic rock hits.

Before leaving the room, she called room service and ordered a salad. One bonus to having an apartment inside a hotel was the ability to call room service whenever she wanted, something she did frequently when she stayed here despite the full kitchen she had, because unlike Gavin, her culinary skills were lacking.

If his plane left California as scheduled, Gavin should arrive at JFK at five. She'd traveled enough to know departure and arrival times changed for a variety of reasons so until he knocked on the door there was no guarantee when he'd get there. Which meant she had a few hours to kill while she waited. She'd recently picked up a novel by her favorite author but hadn't gotten around to starting it. Today seemed like a good time to dive into it.

Curled up on the sofa, she read the last sentence in the paragraph and flipped to the next page. A knock prevented her from reading any more. Since the salad she'd ordered from room service was in the refrigerator, the only other person she expected was Gavin. Sometimes when she read, she lost track of time, but she didn't think she'd been sitting there that long. Setting aside the e-reader, Leah checked her watch. Unless he'd caught an earlier flight out of California, Gavin couldn't be knocking.

She'd never seen or heard of any problems in the hotel, but since it was too soon for it to be Gavin, and she wasn't expecting any other guests, she wasn't going to just open the door either. "Who is it?" she asked.

"Tory," a familiar voice called back.

Tory?

Leah pulled the door open and threw her arms around her second cousin and best friend. She'd seen Tory briefly at Gray's wedding in June. Other than that they hadn't spent any significant time with each other in months. But usually when Tory flew out this way, she called so they could get together.

"When did you get here? And how long are you staying?" Leah asked.

"I got in late last night. My friend's bachelorette party is tonight." She returned Leah's hug. "Unfortunately, I have to leave tomorrow."

If Tory had a party tonight and was leaving in the morning, it didn't leave them much time for visiting. "How did you know I was here?" They hadn't spoken in over two weeks, so Tory had no way of knowing she'd be here instead of Connecticut today.

Tory ran her fingers through her hair—hair Leah had always been jealous of. Instead of being brown or even blonde, Tory had the most gorgeous shade of red Leah had ever seen, a color she'd inherited from her mother.

"I didn't. Since I'm staying in the hotel, I decided to come up and see if you were home."

"Good timing. I spent the weekend at Curt's and only got back a couple hours ago."

Only two weeks apart in age, Leah and Tory had always been good friends despite living on opposite sides on the country. But it wasn't until they'd roomed together at boarding school that their friendship had transcended into almost sisterly.

And like sisters, when they got together they often lost track of time. Today was no different. Tory was in the process of telling Leah about the new house she'd put in an offer on when someone knocked on the door.

Leah glanced down at her watch. Assuming his plane had landed on time and he hadn't run into too much traffic, Gavin should be her newest visitor. "Hold that thought. I'll be right back."

When she opened the door, he didn't give her a chance to even say hello before pulling her close and kissing her as if they'd been apart months rather than a few days. Once he finished kissing her until she could barely stand, he pulled his mouth away and rested his forehead against hers.

"I've missed you," he said in a tone that made her feel cherished and loved.

"Missed you too." Although her body wanted to stay right where it was, they couldn't stand in the doorway all night, especially with Tory there. So while difficult, she stepped away and closed the door. "I'm glad you're back."

WHEN HE TRAVELED he never missed anyone, except perhaps his daughter. But ever since he'd left Leah sleeping in bed on Friday, he'd thought about her and having her in his arms again. Intending to get her back there now, he pulled her against him again, his hands slipping down to her ass as he lowered his lips toward hers. Fortunately, before he made contact and carried out the fantasy playing in his head, he noticed the visitor watching them.

"Act like I'm not even here," the unknown woman called, with a little wave and smile.

He didn't want an audience for what he had in mind.

Moving his hands back to safer ground, he waited for Leah to make introductions.

Stretching up on tiptoes, she put her mouth close to his ear. "I didn't know she was coming by," she whispered so quietly he almost missed it. Then she pulled out of his embrace and turned. "Gavin, this is Tory. I know I've mentioned her a time or two. She's here for a friend's bachelorette party."

Yeah, the woman's name had come up in more than one conversation. Even before their friendship really got going, he'd known Tory Sherbrooke had been the one to introduce Leah to Harry, although he didn't know how Tory and Harry knew each other. He also knew Leah considered the woman her closest friend but didn't see her as much as she'd like because she called the Pacific Coast home.

"Wish I could say she told me about you," Tory commented.

Leaving the apartment was the last thing he wanted to do, but he didn't want to intrude either. "Do you want me to come back later?" he asked.

Tory stood, grabbed an oversized purse from a table, one somehow even bigger than the ones his twin used, and walked toward the door. "No need. I've got to go." She gave him a knowing smile before she hugged Leah, and he almost thanked her. Instead he moved away so they could have some privacy while they said their goodbyes.

"Call me this week." Thanks to his fabulous hearing, he still understood every word she said even though she lowered her voice. "I want to know all about Mr. Hottie over there."

He almost laughed but managed to conceal it with a cough at the last second, causing Leah to look his way.

"Will do," she replied, giving her friend's arm a slight tug. "Gavin, I'll be right back. I'm going to walk Tory to the elevator."

Considering how short a walk it was to the elevator, he expected her back in a minute or two. However, a good ten minutes passed before Leah returned.

"Sorry. I didn't mean to be gone so long." She tried to sit next to him, but he lifted her onto his lap instead. "We got talking," she explained.

He'd never enjoyed simply holding a woman the way he did Leah. They didn't need to be doing anything else. Just having her close filled him with an emotion he couldn't quite identify.

"She wanted to know all about Mr. Hottie waiting for you in here, right?" He tried not to smile, but couldn't manage it.

"You heard her? How?"

Gavin traced her ear with his fingertip. "I have excellent hearing."

Leaving her ear, his finger made a path down her neck and toward the neckline of her V-neck T-shirt. When he reached the lowest point of the V, he moved his fingers under the fabric until his skin brushed against her nipple, already straining against her bra. He teased the nipple for another moment before pulling her shirt up until it cleared her breasts.

Kissing her forehead, he cupped one breasts. "I missed you."

Leah tugged the T-shirt off and let it fall to the floor. "You already told me." She reached behind her back and unclasped the lacy, fire-engine-red bra she was wearing. One he knew would match the lacy thong her shorts were covering because she always wore matching lingerie. "How about you show me?"

~

WITH HIS HEAD in her lap, Gavin closed his eyes and enjoyed

the feel of Leah's fingers going through his hair. Soft music filled the room, and unless a fire broke out, he didn't plan to move from this spot on the sofa anytime soon. He didn't know what time it was and didn't care. The only thing that mattered was he was with her again and would be until tomorrow morning.

"How was your visit with Curt?" She'd informed him of her plans before he left for California but hadn't mentioned it so far tonight.

"Exactly what I needed," she replied.

How do I interpret that one? "That's good," he commented.

Leah's nails gently scratched his scalp before moving down his neck and back up again. "The house still needs a lot of work, but what he's done so far is amazing. I didn't know he'd gotten so good at renovating houses."

"You've never seen his other ones?" Considering the close relationship she shared with her brother, he assumed she'd taken the time to check out his previous projects.

She shook her head. "Only the first one he worked on. He wants us to come and visit. I told him Erin was arriving this week, so it might be awhile before we get there."

As wonderful as the massage felt, if she continued he might fall asleep, so he reached up and took her hands in his. Bringing them to his lips, Gavin kissed her knuckles before settling them on his chest.

"I want to run an idea by you. You said Erin loves art, and I do too. What do you think about her and I spending an afternoon at the Metropolitan Museum of Art or the Museum of Modern Art? If you think there's something she'd rather do, I'm open for suggestions. I thought a day doing something we both liked would be a good way for us to get to know each other." Leah didn't give him a chance to reply before continuing. "But if you don't want us to go on this visit I understand. You haven't seen her in a month. We can do it the next time she comes here."

It took him a moment to fully digest Leah's words. None of the women he'd dated since Erin's mom had showed any interest in even meeting his daughter, and here Leah was proposing she take Erin to an art museum so they could get to know each other.

His chest tightened with emotion and the word love entered his thoughts. "She'll love it. And it'll save me from another museum visit." He took Erin to every museum she mentioned, but he didn't share her interest in art. It was something she inherited from her mom.

Since they were already on the topic of his daughter, he said, "If you can, I want you to come with me when I pick her up at the airport on Friday."

An expression bordering on surprise crossed her face. "Uh, I guess, but wouldn't it be better if you go alone so you can…" She paused for a moment, as if searching for the right word. "…tell her about me."

With the conversation turning serious, Gavin moved into an upright position. "During one of our conversations, I told Erin I wanted her to meet someone special when she got here."

"Oh." Leah rolled her lips together before continuing. "And how did she react?"

"She thought I had finally gotten a puppy. She's been after me for a while to get one. She has a cat at Amber's apartment but really wants a dog." He loved animals but didn't have the time for one. "I explained there wasn't a puppy waiting for her and told her a little about you."

"Talk about a major disappointment for her," Leah commented.

Gavin touched her cheek. "Maybe a little at first, but it passed. She knows the chances of me getting a dog are nonexistent right now. I think she asks more out of habit." He freed her hair from the complicated braid it was in. While she looked great no matter how she did her hair or dressed, he preferred it when she left her hair loose and skipped the makeup, like she had today.

"So will you come on Friday?" he asked again.

This time Leah didn't hesitate to answer. "Of course."

The unidentified emotion filling his chest grew, and he brushed his lips against hers. It was a tender kiss meant to communicate how he felt rather than elicit passion. Eventually Leah pulled back, her eyes sparkling with some unidentifiable emotion. He wondered if it was the same one tugging at his insides.

"Good." The word didn't do justice to his true thoughts, but it was the best he could come up with. He'd never had a woman in his life during any of Erin's previous visits. Finding the right balance between time with Erin alone as well as Erin and Leah might take some time and effort. But Leah was worth it.

"It's going to be different with Erin here, but I need to see you too," he continued.

"No need to explain. I know the next two weeks are all about Erin and that you'll want time alone time with her. Just tell me when and where and I'll be there."

Maybe someday he'd have to thank his half brother for being such an ass, because if Harry hadn't cheated on Leah, she might not be sitting here with him now. "You're amazing, you know."

He wasn't trying to get brownie points or anything. The compliment just slipped out because it was true. Leah Sherbrooke was the most understanding woman he knew.

If they weren't sitting so close, he would've missed the slight blush across her cheeks.

"I'll take your word for it. But seriously, since I'm not

traveling for work again until October, I have some flexibility, so whenever you want me around, I should be able to make it."

Officially he had Erin's first week in New York off. He'd structured it so that during her second week with him, he should only have to spend a few hours a day working from home. And unless something unexpected came up, those could be hours when Erin was sleeping.

"Stay with us while she's here."

Before they'd started spending nights together, Gavin often had trouble sleeping. More nights than not, he stared at the ceiling for hours before drifting off to a restless sleep. On the nights Leah was next to him, it wasn't an issue. The first few times he thought it was a coincidence that he slept well with her there. The few times before his recent business trip he'd slept alone and then the two nights in California without Leah proved he simply slept better with her there.

A better night's sleep wasn't the only reason he wanted her with him. When she was around he felt content in a way he'd never experienced before. Maybe it was selfish, but he didn't want to deprive himself of it for the next two weeks.

"I planned on giving you a key this week anyway," he continued. Other than Harry, he'd never given anyone the key to his condo. But he wanted Leah to think of his place as another home.

THE SUBJECT of whether they'd be spending nights together had crossed her mind numerous times over the weekend. And although Curt suggested she ask Gavin about it, she'd decided to wait and let him bring up the topic.

"You don't think she'll find it weird I'm sleeping in your bedroom?"

"Why would she?" Gavin asked.

In all the months Leah had known him, she'd never known him to date. Gavin's response made her wonder if he'd had other woman spend the night when his daughter was with him in New York.

She shrugged slightly before answering. "Curt said they make sure Reese never sees Taylor coming out of his room when they stay at his place in Newport. I thought maybe you wouldn't want Erin to know we shared a room either."

But hey, if she's used to seeing a woman come out of your bedroom.... Leah forced her train of thought to stop before she said something inappropriate. Because whom Gavin had been involved with before her wasn't any of her business, and it wasn't like she hadn't dated or slept with other men before they met either.

"Amber's fiancé spends more time at their apartment than his own. Erin sees him coming out her mom's bedroom all the time. It's never happened when she's been here, but I don't think it'll faze Erin if she knows you sleep in my room."

She'd had more than a couple boyfriends. During those relationships she'd sometimes spent a night at their house or they'd stay with her. When they weren't together, she'd never cared. With Gavin it was different. In a very short amount of time, she'd grown used to having him in bed next to her. She loved falling asleep with his arm around her and waking up in the middle of the night and just knowing he slept inches away. When she woke up in the morning, having him there made getting ready for the day much more enjoyable too.

"As long as you think Erin will be okay with it, I'll stay with you," she responded.

She considered his comment about giving her a key to his condo. Even though she'd never given a boyfriend a key to her home, she'd been considering it since before he left for California, and had even pulled a spare one from her desk drawer. In the end she'd decided to hold off another week or two before saying anything, worried Gavin might interpret the gesture to mean she wanted more of a commitment from him.

"I dug out a spare key to my house for you too," she admitted. "I don't have one for here, but I'll talk to hotel security about getting one for you."

For the next half hour or so, Gavin shared the plans he had in mind for his daughter's stay. He'd included everything from a trip to the Above The Trees Adventure obstacle course and Paradise Fairway, to a concert at Madison Square Garden by one of Erin's favorite musicians and a baseball game. Considering everything he had planned, the young girl might sleep for a month straight once she returned to her mom in Providence. Heck, Leah was tired from just listening to the list. And although she thought it might be a little too much, even without asking she understood why he wanted to get as much in as possible. His time with Erin was limited, and he wanted to make it as memorable for both of them as possible.

Eventually, Gavin finished explaining his plans for Erin's visit, and she took the opportunity to inquire about his time with Vivian. Other than the fact that the woman was ten minutes older than Gavin and lived in California, Leah knew very little about his twin sister.

"It shocked the hell out of me when Jeffrey Moore showed up."

He said the name as if she knew who the man was, but it didn't sound at all familiar to her.

"Is he an actor?" she asked. Since his sister lived in California, the home of Hollywood, it was a plausible guess.

Gavin shook his head. "Soccer player. He plays for Bay City United. He was also on the US soccer team in the 2016 Summer Olympics."

Except for baseball and the occasional New England

Rebels football game, she didn't follow professional sports. If he watched enough soccer to know the players who'd competed for the United States in the Olympics, he did more than watch an occasional game. She'd have to brush up on the sport. Maybe she could enlist Reese's aid.

"Viv stays away from athletes," he continued. "She turned down both Drew McKenzie and CJ Major."

Now those were two names she recognized. Star players on the New England Rebels football team, they'd both appeared on numerous commercials and genuinely sounded like nice men. Drew McKenzie was married now, but if either he or CJ had asked her out prior to meeting Gavin, she would've agreed.

"Sometimes the type of person you're attracted to changes," she suggested. "And nothing against soccer or Jeffrey Moore, but he doesn't fall in the same category as Drew and CJ. Maybe your sister just didn't want to be involved with someone so well-known. Neither of them can probably go anywhere without being recognized. Trust me, being with someone so recognizable can get annoying. And the media loves to use their pictures and whoever they're with on magazine covers."

She'd inherited her dad's Sherbrooke blue eyes and light hair, but otherwise she took more after her mom, so most people didn't immediately recognize her as a Sherbrooke. It also helped she'd gone out of her way to stay off the media's radar. Her brother Curt and several of her cousins, especially Trent and Jake thanks to their reputations before they both married, weren't as fortunate, and people recognized them everywhere. She loved her family, but on occasion, going anywhere with them wasn't worth the hassle.

"Last year Vivian dated Anderson Brady for a few months, and before him she was with Malcolm Stewart," he explained, referring to two well-known A-list actors. "The attention doesn't bother her. But ever since sophomore year of college, she doesn't get involved with athletes. Or she hasn't until now."

If Vivian had sworn off an entire group of men, something significant must have occurred in college. Although curious, Leah didn't ask for specifics because it wasn't any of her business.

"Every August, Vivian comes for Piper's birthday. This year she's going to try to get here a littler earlier since Erin will be here. She told me to make sure you're around when she visits. She wants to fill you in on all my most embarrassing moments."

Leah rubbed her hands together in anticipation. "I can hardly wait."

ELEVEN

If a person's mood could be improved by simply touching another human being, every soul inside the airport having a bad day should shake Gavin's hand. Happiness radiated off him tonight. It had actually been there since they woke up this morning. While they shared their first cups of coffee of the day, Leah thought his mood couldn't get any more jubilant.

She'd been wrong.

If this morning he'd been as excited and happy as a child about to meet Santa Claus, tonight his mood reflected that of a child about to meet Santa, the Tooth Fairy, and the Easter Bunny all at once. Leah didn't think she'd ever been quite as happy as he was in her entire life, and she'd had some wonderful and exciting experiences over the past thirty-two years.

The arm around her waist tightened as they entered the airport. As usual, it was bustling with activity. Gavin guided them through the crowd toward the large screens listing the arrivals and departures. The airport was a great place to people watch, so while he checked for information regarding Erin's flight, she focused on everyone around them.

"First they charge me twenty-five dollars to check my bag, and then they lose it," a woman to Leah's right said to her companion. The couple had two preteens with them, both of whom wore earbuds and were staring down at their cell phones, completely ignoring their parents. "I'm starting to wish we'd gone camping again instead of coming here," the woman grumbled.

Too bad Gavin couldn't transfer some of his happiness, because this woman needed a large helping of it.

"Before we pick up the rental car, I need a coffee," the unhappy traveler said.

"There is a snack stand over there," her companion replied.

Leah watched the family head toward the stand. Considering the woman's attitude, the evening facing her companions looked unpleasant, and Leah was glad she wasn't part of the small group.

"Looks like their flight is expected to arrive on time," Gavin said, and the word *their* in his statement immediately caught her attention.

Children could fly without an adult. When she traveled on commercial airlines rather than private charter flights, she occasionally saw a child alone. An airline employee usually escorted them on and off the plane and then a family member met them somewhere in the airport. Since Erin was coming directly from Florida and her mom lived in Rhode Island, she'd assumed Erin was traveling alone while Amber returned home.

She let him lead her away from the screens and toward one of the busy coffee shops inside the airport. "Is Erin's mom with her?"

"Both Amber and her fiancé are with Erin. We don't let

her travel alone. Todd, Amber's fiancé, has family in the city. They're going to visit with them before returning to Providence on Sunday." They entered the coffee shop and headed straight for the last empty table. After pulling out a chair, Gavin waited for her to sit. "What would you like?"

"Whatever you're having," Leah replied, her thoughts focused solely on what he'd shared. She had prepared to meet Erin today, not Amber. While meeting new people never bothered her—actually, she enjoyed it—the thought of meeting the woman Gavin had at one time loved enough to have a child with set her nerves on edge.

It doesn't matter if she likes me. Even as she thought it, Leah realized the statement was only partially true. While Amber's feeling regarding her wouldn't affect her and Gavin's relationship, it could cause problems between her and Gavin's daughter. Growing up, she'd had enough friends with divorced parents to know that the other parent often influenced a child's opinion of a new boyfriend or girlfriend. If Amber didn't like her, her opinion could easily rub off on Erin, causing some very uncomfortable situations during future visits.

Gavin set a covered paper cup and a blueberry scone in front of her. "You look deep in thought. Everything okay?" Rather than sit across from her, he pulled out the chair next to her.

"Yep." Afraid he'd see the truth, she uncovered the cup without meeting his eyes. "Just lost in thought."

He did the same and added two packets of sugar to the mocha-colored liquid in the cup. "Did you get a hold of your cousin?"

"I'm going to spend the day with her."

With tomorrow being Gavin and Erin's first day together in weeks, it seemed only right they had the time alone. Since they'd be gone most of the day, she'd made plans to spend time with Callie and her family.

Lifting the cup, she paused with it near her lips. "Do you and Amber's fiancé get along?" If the man was at Amber's apartment more than his own, Gavin must have run into him often. Even if he didn't spend so much time there, Gavin would've made a point of meeting the man who spent time around his daughter.

"Todd isn't someone I'd call to go hang out with, but yeah, we get along. He's a decent guy. Amber and he are a good fit, and he treats Erin like a princess. I think he spoils her worse than I do."

Gavin checked his watch every two seconds as they enjoyed their coffees and chatted about their day—or at least it seemed like every two seconds. Finally after what had to be the twentieth time, he stuffed his napkin in his empty coffee cup and pushed back his chair. "Ready?"

Half her latte remained, so she put the cover back on the cup and stood. Reaching out, she laced his fingers with her own. "I'll finish on the way."

They waited near the terminal exit as travelers walked past them, some alone and others in small groups. She'd not only seen the pictures Gavin had of Erin on his cell phone, she'd also seen the ones he kept in his home office and the one in his bedroom of them together. So she immediately recognized the young girl headed in their direction.

"She's a mini you," Leah commented.

She thought the girl resembled Gavin in pictures, but in person it was even more evident. From here she couldn't tell the exact shade of Erin's eyes, but her hair color matched Gavin's to a T, and the shape of their faces was the same. She shared Gavin's height as well. If Leah didn't know any different, she'd easily assume Erin was eleven or twelve years old.

Leah switched her gaze to the two adults accompanying

Erin. Amber was tall like her daughter and willowy, with light brown hair and a heart-shaped face. As they walked, she held Erin's hand and listened to whatever her daughter was saying. Todd, Amber's fiancé, looked vaguely familiar, but from where remained just out of Leah's reach.

Everyone in the airport terminal knew the exact moment Erin spotted her father.

"Dad," the girl shouted, and sprinted away from her mom. Her smile radiated so much happiness it was almost blinding.

Erin launched herself into Gavin's arms and he picked her up off the ground. The smile on his face matched his daughter's. "How's my girl?" he asked before kissing her on the cheek and setting her back down.

Although he no longer hugged her, Gavin put an arm over Erin's shoulders.

"Hungry. Can we get pizza on the way home? Or Chinese?"

He'd warned her that Erin would happily live on only pizza, grilled cheese sandwiches, and Chinese food if allowed. She hadn't told him, but when she was about Erin's age those had been her favorite food groups too. Even now pizza with a large helping of ice cream afterward were her go-to dishes when she needed some comfort food.

"We'll see, Bug," he replied as Amber and Todd reached them.

Gavin's fingers wrapped around hers and gave them a quick squeeze before he stepped forward and gave Amber a brief friendly hug. After releasing her, Gavin turned toward Todd. "Congratulations on the engagement," he said, shaking Todd's hand before he moved back to her side, his arm immediately going around her shoulders.

Quickly Gavin went through introductions before they all started toward the baggage claim area. As they walked, he kept her hand locked in his right hand while his left held his daughter's. Erin entertained them with details of her vacation, starting with the flight down to Florida weeks ago. By the time they reached the baggage area, she'd only made it through the first two days of the trip.

LEAH STOOD by his side and his daughter was within arm's reach. The only thing that could make the moment better was if they weren't standing inside the airport. But at least they wouldn't be here much longer. He had Erin's two suitcases in hand, and Erin was in the process of saying bye to Amber and Todd.

Erin gave first her mom and then Todd a hug before turning and skipping back to his side, the unicorn-shaped backpack Todd had carried off the plane for her slung over one shoulder.

"Do you need to use the bathroom before we go?" She'd insisted she didn't have to when her mom had asked on their way to get their luggage. Since the ladies' room was right across from them now and he'd rather not have her announce ten minutes after they got in the car that she needed to go, he asked again.

"Nope. I went on the plane."

Some things he could force her to do; using the bathroom wasn't one of them. "Okay, this way then."

Erin spent a lot more time at his apartment in Providence than here, but she knew her way around. When they walked in, she immediately dropped her backpack on the floor and zipped down the hall to the bathroom.

The anticipated announcement that she needed to go had come fifteen rather than ten minutes into their ride home, but it had still come. It had taken considerable effort not to remind her that he'd asked before they left the airport.

While Erin used the bathroom, he brought her bright

yellow suitcases and backpack down to the guest bedroom she used whenever she visited. Unlike her room at his other home, which she'd helped decorate, this one was an identical copy of the one across the hall, right down to the dark gray comforter and bare hardwood floor. During her last visit in April, she'd asked if they could make this room more like her one in Providence. He'd promised they could, but they'd been so busy with other activities they never got around to shopping.

Until now, he hadn't thought about her request since.

Gavin made a mental note to get some shopping in while she was here so she could change things up in the room and switched off the light.

He met up with Erin in the hallway as she came out of the bathroom. "Where's Uncle Harry?" she asked.

When it came to romantic relationships, Harry could be a first-class bastard, but he was a good uncle, and the last time Erin stayed here, Harry was living with him. During that week Harry had been on his best behavior. He hadn't brought home any women, and he'd spent several hours playing video games with Erin.

"He's not living here anymore. His new house is done."

She slipped her hand into his, a gesture he never tired of, while they walked back to the living room. "When will we see him?"

Unless away on vacation, Harry always made a point to see Erin at least once when she was in New York. Two months ago Gavin would've reminded his half brother Erin was arriving today. Given his relationship with Leah, he'd kept silent about Erin's upcoming visit, hoping to avoid an unexpected visit from Harry while Leah was around.

"Not sure, Bug. We'll have to wait and see."

"I made him a bracelet. I made one for you too, and it looks just like mine." She held up her wrist so he could see the black and yellow friendship bracelet tied around it. "They're in my backpack."

Erin left him with little choice. "I'll call him later and see if he's around." And if Harry did visit, Gavin would make sure Leah knew beforehand so she could go elsewhere if she wanted.

Satisfied with his response, she moved on to another topic. "Can we get pizza tonight?"

They did need to eat, but he wasn't in the mood for pizza. Honestly, he didn't know what he wanted, but he knew it wasn't pizza. "Let's see what Leah feels likes and then decide."

Erin flopped into an armchair across from Leah and folded her legs up like a pretzel. "Are you and Leah going to get married like Mom and Todd?"

You had to ask me that now. Part of being a parent was embarrassing questions from your child. And he'd gotten plenty of them from Erin since she first learned to talk. This one got the gold medal, though.

Leah cleared her throat, and when he shot a quick look at her, she had a hand over her mouth. When their eyes met, she merely shrugged and remained silent.

Thanks for the help.

"Your mom and Todd have known each other a lot longer than Leah and me." The reply didn't answer Erin's question, but it wasn't a lie either. Before she could point out he hadn't given her the information she wanted, he spoke again. "Bug wants pizza. I'm leaning more toward Thai or Indian. What are you in the mood for, Leah?"

When Leah dropped her hand into her lap, a smile tugged at her lips. "Pizza gets my vote."

DURING DINNER and as they played a friendly board game, Gavin found himself mentally stepping back and watching Leah and Erin interact. Somehow Leah seemed to ask his daughter all the right questions. In no time they were chatting away as if Leah had known Erin since birth and completely ignoring him.

He knew it was a good sign that they were getting along well already, but that didn't mean he liked being the odd man out where his daughter was concerned.

"She reminds me of Reese," Leah commented.

They were alone for the first time since leaving the airport. He'd sent Erin to change into pajamas before they put on one of her favorite superhero movies. For the past year or so she'd been obsessed with superheroes, especially female ones. Before that she'd been into movies based on her favorite book series. No doubt in another year or so, she'd have a new obsession.

"I thought the same thing when we were at your brother's house."

Leaning closer, he touched his lips to hers in the briefest of kisses and then pulled away. Regardless of his best intentions, sometimes when he meant to merely kiss Leah, desire got the better of him and he got carried away. Yeah, they were alone now, but Erin could return at any moment, and he didn't want her walking in on anything inappropriate.

"She likes you already." Leah might not be a mother, but she was a natural with his daughter. "Todd and Erin get along great now, but I remember Amber telling me it took Todd a good month of trying before Erin warmed up to him."

"Must be because I voted for pizza tonight."

He pretended to consider Leah's theory. "It probably helped," he agreed with a straight face. "But it's not the only reason." Gavin was about to tell Leah how much he appreciated the way she was welcoming his daughter into her life, but a tornado of energy disguised as a young girl in pastel-colored pjs stopped him.

Erin flung herself on the sofa next to him. "Here's your bracelet." She handed him a larger version of the one she wore. "Mom let me bring the thread with me. I'll make you one tomorrow, Leah. Do you like yellow and black? I have pink, purple, and green thread too. I made Uncle Harry a green and black one. What colors would you like?"

"Surprise me," Leah replied.

Satisfied with the answer, Erin settled in next to him and leaned her head against his arm as he pressed Play on the remote control. Immediately, the theme song to the newest superhero movie in the series filled the room. Once the action started, Erin wouldn't say much of anything else.

But the action on the screen hadn't started yet.

"My room is ugly. You promised we could change it. Can we do it tomorrow?"

"I planned to take you to Six Flags in the morning. How about I take you sometime next week?" The weather for the next few days looked great for outdoor excursions, and he didn't get many opportunities to enjoy the outdoors. If he had to go shopping, an activity he didn't care for, he'd rather do it on a day when it was better to stay inside anyway.

"Or I can take you," Leah offered. She knew his views on shopping. "We can make it a girls' day out. Visit the Met first, have some lunch, and then go shopping."

During dinner Leah had discussed art with Erin, and he'd expected to her to ask Erin then if she'd like to visit a museum with her. She hadn't.

"I love the Met. Can we go Sunday?" Erin asked.

"Your dad has something planned for Sunday. But I'll take the day off and we can go Tuesday."

I love you. The thought formed before the magnitude of it hit him like a high-speed train.

He didn't enjoy spending time with Leah.

He didn't desire her.

He *loved* her.

How could he not? Not only was she thoughtful and caring, but she was also making Erin a part of her life and saving him from a shopping trip.

He should've realized it days ago, because the emotion pulling at his heart now was the same one he'd experienced on Sunday night.

"Awesome. I can't wait."

Now that the opening sequence was over, Erin turned her attention to the television. With her eyes focused solely on the movie, he brushed a kiss across Leah's cheek. Later, when they were alone, he'd demonstrate his gratitude. But for now words would have to suffice.

"Thank you," he whispered before relaxing and simply enjoying the moment with the two people in the world most important to him.

TWELVE

Weekends went by fast, especially in the summer, but the past one had literally gone by in a blur. It seemed as if one minute Leah was enjoying breakfast with Gavin and Erin Saturday morning before she left for her cousin's house, and then the next she was waking up for work this morning.

Unfortunately, the workday hadn't passed anywhere near as quickly as the weekend. Leah couldn't put all the blame on the fact that it was a Monday and in general Mondays were her least favorite day of the week. Nope, the blame rested squarely on her shoulders. Needing to cram two days' worth of work into one, she headed into the office long before she usually did and stayed there several hours later. Actually, her Monday resembled the workdays Gavin put in on a regular basis. Or more accurately, the days he'd put in before their weekend in Newport.

Since then he spent fewer hours at Culloden headquarters, although he still did extra work when he got home. Most often he did it in the early morning hours before the sun came up, when he thought she was sleeping. Not that Gavin was aware that she knew. But more than once she'd woken up to get a drink or to use the bathroom and discovered him gone. The first time it happened she left the bedroom, only to see the lights on in his office down the hall. She'd been tempted to go inside and ask him to come back to bed.

But she hadn't.

Well before their first kiss, she'd known he put in more time at work in a week than some people did in a month. If getting things done while he thought she was sleeping was his way of making sure they had more time together, she wouldn't interfere.

At least for now.

Eventually the missed sleep might catch up to him. If it did, she would say something, but until then she'd mind her own business on this one.

Unlocking the door, she walked inside expecting to hear the television or Erin's voice as she talked Gavin's ear off. It had certainly been the case on Saturday when she returned to his place after visiting Callie and her family. And on Sunday when Leah met up with them in the building lobby, Erin had talked nonstop from the moment the elevator doors closed until they sat down for dinner.

Silence greeted her tonight instead.

Kicking off her heels, she picked them up and crossed into the living room, where she switched on a table lamp. "Hello," she called, on the off chance they were home.

An unanticipated reply came from down the hallway. "In my office."

He'd taken the week off to spend with his daughter. Even next week he'd arranged it so he could devote most of his time to Erin. So what was he doing in his office tonight? Shouldn't the two of them be enjoying a snack or playing a video game?

Strolling through the open door, she found Gavin seated at his desk dressed in a sleeveless T-shirt. She couldn't make out the words, but a document was up on his home computer and his laptop was powered on as well. His briefcase sat open next to a picture of Erin with his younger sister Piper on the credenza behind him

"Hey, you," she greeted. "Is Erin sleeping?" Being only seven o'clock it seemed unlikely she'd be asleep, but Gavin had taken Erin hiking today. Maybe hiking on a hot summer day was what it took to tire out his daughter. Nothing else seemed to.

His fingers paused over the keyboard and he looked up at her. "Nope, she's not home. Gigi showed up before we left this morning. She insisted on taking Erin for the day. She hasn't seen Erin since Christmas."

"And you immediately came in here?" She leaned her hip against the side of his desk.

Rolling his chair back, Gavin reached for her, pulling her closer until she stood between his legs. "No. I took care of a few errands I've been putting off. And I picked up a birthday present for my sister while I was out too." His hands on her waist slipped around to the small of her back. "My dad called. Piper wants to celebrate her birthday early so Erin can come to the party. Instead of the party being on her birthday, it's going to be next weekend."

Considering the close friendship he'd explained existed between the two girls, Piper's request seemed natural.

"I told him Erin and I would be there. I'd like you to come with us." He cleared his throat before he continued. "But I understand if you'd rather skip it. Harry will most be likely there. Unless he's out of state, he doesn't miss Piper's birthday parties."

She had no desire to be in the same room with Harry Kincaid again. Unfortunately, the man was Gavin's half brother, so unless they put an end to their relationship tomorrow, the possibility of going the rest of her life without seeing

Harry again was almost nonexistent. So while she appreciated the gesture, skipping Piper's birthday party would only delay the evitable.

"Harry or no Harry, I'll come with you. I'll have Erin help me find a present for Piper when we go shopping tomorrow." Nothing was more embarrassing than showing up at a birthday party empty-handed.

Without warning he stood and lifted her onto the edge of his desk. His fingers brushed against the bare skin just below the hem of her skirt before he pushed the fabric up until it reached almost where leg met torso, allowing her to open her legs further.

When she did, he moved in between them. The hard ridge behind his zipper pressed into her. Closing her eyes, she took in slow, deep breaths, simply enjoying the feel of him against her.

One of his hands trailed up and over her waist before settling on her right breast. His touch burned through her blouse, setting her skin on fire. On their own, her fingers moved to the tiny buttons holding the top closed and began undoing each one.

"When will Erin be back?" It was the first time since Friday morning they'd been alone, and she was suddenly desperate to have his hands and mouth everywhere.

The hand still resting on her thigh moved up and under her skirt. "No idea," he admitted, his fingers pushing aside her panties and then moving against her, causing her muscles to contract as she pressed into his hand.

With her blouse no longer buttoned, he spread the two sides apart with his other hand and yanked her bra down, exposing one breast. "Don't worry, they'll ring the doorbell." His teeth raked across her nipple as his finger sank inside her, making it impossible to offer up a reply.

He teased and stroked until Leah thought she'd die from

pleasure. Needing to finally have him inside her, she reached for the button on his shorts.

Or at least she tried.

Gavin brushed her hand away. “Not yet. I’m not done.”

Before she could argue, he dropped to his knees between her legs and proceeded to love her with his tongue and lips until she grabbed his shoulders to keep from flying off the desk.

Only after she’d touched the stars and started to drift back down to earth did he stand and she heard his zipper move. “I love you,” Gavin said near her ear.

The words hit her heart and spread through her soul. Opening her eyes, she met his steady gaze. His eyes burned with the same heat and desire she’d seen before, but now they reflected love too. And she didn’t need a mirror to know the same emotions shone brightly in her eyes.

“I love you too.”

DROPPING the L-word tonight hadn’t been on his agenda. Hell, he’d only realized the truth recently and his feelings had run much deeper than mere friendship for months. So the chances of her sharing the sentiment so soon in their relationship seemed unlikely. But when she agreed to go with him and Erin to the party even though Harry would be there, keeping the words back had been impossible.

“Should I let you get back to work?” Leah asked. At the moment she sat in his lap; her blouse remained unbuttoned but much to his disappointment she’d readjusted her bra.

Yeah, like he’d get any more done in here tonight. He might never get work done in his office again. Every time he walked in, the memory of bringing her to orgasm on his desk before making love to her would occupy his thoughts.

Her lips were still red and swollen from kissing and Gavin couldn't resist tasting her again. "I've got all day tomorrow while you and Erin are gone," he explained once his lips left hers.

Leah's hand skimmed across his shoulder and around to the back of his neck. Her fingertips brushed back and forth against his skin. "Since you missed out on the day with Erin, are you sure you still want us to go? The museum will be there next week."

"She'd never forgive me if I canceled your girls' day out. It was all she talked about yesterday," he replied. "I'll take her hiking later in the week."

Smiling, she kissed his cheek. "I might not forgive you either. I haven't been on a good shopping spree in months."

Shopping spree? Leah had promised to help Erin pick out things for her bedroom. He envisioned that to mean a new comforter and maybe some of those throw pillows women loved so much. It sounded like Leah had much more in mind.

"Don't go nuts tomorrow."

She feigned an innocent expression, one he wasn't buying for a second.

"Never. But I saw Erin's room. It's not a girl's bedroom. It looks like a room at some hotel. It needs a facelift, my dear." She patted the back of his neck.

He couldn't argue with Leah's assessment. Erin's room and the other spare bedroom both lacked character. "Just bring me back the receipts for whatever you buy."

He'd gladly hand the chore of shopping off to Leah, but he'd pick up the cost. This was his house and his daughter.

"We'll see," she replied.

The doorbell rang, preventing him from pressing the issue.

Slipping off his lap, Leah buttoned up her blouse and then straightened her skirt. "How's my hair?" she asked.

Despite their activities, only a few blonde strands had escaped the twist she'd pulled her hair into that morning. Nothing about it would suggest to his grandmother or anyone else what they'd been up to.

Her top was another story. The back was no longer tucked into her skirt and it had more wrinkles than a full-grown Neapolitan Mastiff. "Your hair is fine."

At eighty-two, Jean Kincaid had more energy than most women half her age. The woman simply never stopped. When she wasn't experimenting in her kitchen or traveling around the world, she was playing tennis or skiing. And although she had spent an entire day entertaining a nine-year-old, she looked wide-awake and ready to tackle anything.

"Sorry it's so late." Gigi hugged him before handing him several bags from various stores. "We did a little shopping for my upcoming cruise and then we started cooking. We both lost track of time."

Judging by the bags he was holding, they hadn't shopped only for Gigi's upcoming trip.

"Erin knows her way around the kitchen already," his grandmother continued.

Before he could tell Gigi that he and Erin often cooked together, she turned her eyes in Leah's direction. "You must be Leah. Erin talked about you all day. I hoped to meet you tonight."

While Gigi led Leah off toward the sofa, her mouth going a mile a minute, a trait she'd passed on to his daughter, Gavin turned his attention to Erin. When she'd left that morning, she'd been wearing a pair of jean shorts and a T-shirt with a unicorn on the front. Now she had on a one-piece romper—or at least he thought that was what the outfit was called. Although she looked adorable, it wasn't the type of clothes she usually picked.

"Did Gigi pick that out?" He gestured toward her clothes.

Erin nodded. "She got me a purple one like it. And I picked out the clothes she has on."

He'd noticed his grandmother was wearing a different outfit as well. And if Erin had picked it out, he never would've guessed because it was just as vibrant as all the other clothes Gigi favored. As far as Gigi was concerned, there was no such thing as too bright. She loved bold colors and animal prints. If anyone tried to tell her she was too old to wear either, they got an earful.

"She got me a bunch of other outfits. I'll show you." Erin reached for one of the bags he held.

"Tomorrow. Right now it's time for bed."

Erin offered up a few grumbles. Even as a baby she'd disliked going to sleep, and the older she got the more she resisted, especially if she thought she'd miss out on something. Like tonight, with both her great-grandmother and Leah chatting in the living room.

After a good ten minutes of dragging her feet, first by insisting she needed a glass of water, then in the bathroom, and finally getting changed, Gavin pulled the blankets up and over her.

Leaning down, he kissed her forehead. "See you in the morning, Bug. I love you."

When he returned, Leah and his grandmother remained in conversation, but they weren't sitting down. A good sign, because if Gigi planned to make this a long visit, she would've sat down and made herself comfortable.

"Just waiting for you to come back before I left," Gigi said when she caught sight of him.

Good. He loved Gigi, but tonight he wasn't in the mood for entertaining visitors.

"Are the three of you going to Piper's party?" she asked.

"We'll be there. Vivian too," Gavin replied.

"Excellent. I'll see you both then." Gigi said her goodbyes and left.

No sooner had the door closed than he pulled out the clips holding Leah's hair up. He raked his fingers through the strands, content to stand there and do nothing else but touch her hair.

"She's not exactly what I expected," Leah stated. "Is she always so full of life? I thought my grandmother had a lot of energy, but I think yours could run circles around mine. I got tired just talking to her."

"More or less." Gavin pulled his hands from her hair, reached for the top button of her blouse, and released it. "If you're tired, I can tuck you into bed now too." He unfastened the second and third buttons.

Tonight in his office was the first time they'd been intimate since Erin arrived. But not making love to Leah again now might kill him. "It's up to you." He slid his hand across her chest and into her bra.

Before she answered, he grazed her nipple with his fingertip and lowered his mouth to hers in time to catch her groan.

THIRTEEN

Leah loved art. She always had. Some of her favorite childhood memories were of strolling through art museums with her mom. She didn't care if the pieces were completed during the Renaissance period or the late twentieth century; she enjoyed it all. Of all the museums she visited, the Metropolitan Museum of Art was at the top of her list, followed closely by the National Gallery in London and, of course, the Louvre. What art lover didn't like the Louvre?

Somehow, today, going through the various collections housed in the museum was different. She'd seen many of the paintings and sculptures countless times, but this morning with Erin it'd been like seeing them for the first time. Gavin's daughter reminded Leah of herself when she'd visited museums with her mom. She pointed out her favorite pieces and had no qualms about telling Leah which ones she thought were hideous. Oddly, many of the ones Erin disliked, she didn't care for either. Leah wisely kept the opinion to herself. They'd already earned more than one disgruntled look thanks to Erin's comments.

After a few hours of strolling through first the modern

and contemporary art, and then the medieval displays, they made their way to the American Wing. Judging by Erin's comments, it was her favorite of the three. They finished their visit to the museum with lunch at the café and a quick stop at the gift shop. As a kid, no visit to the museum had been complete for Leah without a stop there. Erin felt the same way.

She took her time walking through the store and checking out the various items offered before picking out two posters to hang on her bedroom wall. Once finished, they left for the only store in the city Leah visited when she wanted to add or change something in a room but didn't want to wait for anything to be custom made.

"What do you want to look for first?" Leah asked. When she shopped, she liked to have a plan rather than wandering around aimlessly until she spotted something she liked.

Aside from painting the walls and buying new furniture, Gavin had given them permission to change anything they wanted in the room. If it were her bedroom, the dark gray comforter would be the first thing to go, along with the matching curtains. Even now she tended to stay away from anything in the gray family, and it had definitely never appeared in her room when she'd been younger. Considering the colors she'd seen Erin wear, Gavin's daughter preferred fun, vibrant colors, and gray was not vibrant no matter the shade.

"Stuff for my bed. I hate gray; it's super boring. Everything on my bed at Mom's is yellow. And at dad's other apartment I have a lot of rainbows and mermaids in my room."

"Is yellow your favorite color?" Some shades of yellow were nice, but when it came to decorating, it wasn't a color she went with. But this wasn't her bedroom, so if Erin wanted yellow, they'd look for anything and everything in yellow.

Together they stepped off the escalator and walked toward

the bedding section of the store. "It used to be. Now I like purple and pink more. Mom said when she decorates the other bedroom for the baby she'll let me change my room too. She promised I can help pick stuff out, but we have to wait until we know if the baby is a boy or a girl."

The woman she'd met at the airport hadn't looked pregnant. If she was expecting, she couldn't be much further along than Callie, who'd told her over the weekend that she was pregnant with her second baby.

"Do you want a brother or a sister?" Leah asked. The sex of a baby might not matter to parents or grandparents, but all children had a preference when it came to new siblings.

Erin proved to be no different.

"A sister. My cousin Spencer is a year older than me, and he's so mean. He always picks on me. I'm glad he lives in Florida so I don't have to see him much. Do you have any sisters?"

They entered an area filled with sheets, pillows, and comforters designed with children and preteens in mind. Nearly everything was covered with cartoon animals, superheroes, or emoji symbols, including a giant pillow in the shape of poop. Whatever else Erin picked out today, Leah hoped that pillow wasn't among the items. Or anything else with a poop emoji on it, for that matter.

"No, two older brothers. But I have a lot of female cousins and we're close. Almost like sisters."

Erin walked down the aisle looking at the various sheet sets, and Leah was relieved when she walked by the ones sporting the crazy emoji symbols.

"Are your brothers mean like Spencer?" She picked up a sheet set decorated with panda bears, considered it for a moment, and then returned it to the shelf.

"Nah, annoying sometimes but not mean. If you have a brother, I'm sure you'll get along." Spotting a comforter with a unicorn print, Leah grabbed it. Erin had a unicorn-shaped backpack, so it was a safe guess she liked unicorns. "What do you think?"

Erin was about to pick up a tie-dyed sheet set but her hand dropped back to her side when she saw what Leah was holding. "I love it. Can we see if they have stuff to match it?"

Leah nodded and together they went in search of anything and everything unicorn. She didn't know Gavin's opinion on unicorns, but she assumed he'd prefer it to many of the other options on display.

"A baby brother might be okay. I'll be older than him, so he won't be able to pick on me like Spencer. But I still really want a sister." Gavin's daughter grabbed three unicorn-shaped throw pillows, each with a different-colored mane, and added them to what they'd already selected. "Are you and Dad going to have a baby like Mom and Todd?"

Curt was right. He'd told her to be prepared for some entertaining conversations while Erin was around. Getting asked if she planned to have children was more embarrassing than entertaining, but considering what they'd been discussing, maybe it shouldn't surprise her.

Yet it did. And now she had to answer the question.

"If you do, maybe I'll have two sisters," Erin continued, oblivious to the fact Leah had stopped moving. "But I guess if Mom has a boy and you have a boy I could get two brothers." She paused as if thinking about it before continuing. "Or maybe if you and Dad have a baby they'll be twins like Dad and Aunt Vivian. That would be cool."

First Erin had her having one baby and now she was talking about twins. Had she discussed this topic with Gavin too? If so, how had he handled it?

"I wish I had a twin sister. My two best friends in school are identical twins and they're always playing tricks on people. Even their mom and dad get them mixed up sometimes. We had a sleepover on the last day of school and all night Ava's mom thought she was Kasey and Kasey was Ava. But I knew who was who."

Maybe if she kept Erin talking about her friends, she'd forget about her earlier question regarding whether she could expect a second brother or sister in the future.

"Tricking people does sound like fun. Are they on your soccer team?"

Erin nodded. "Their dad is our coach, and their cousin is on the team too." They passed by a display of table lamps and Erin stopped. "This one matches the unicorn's hair." She pointed at a light with a bright aqua-colored lampshade.

Thank you.

If Erin was again focused on redecorating her room, she didn't need to answer her question about babies or hopefully anything else pertaining to her and Gavin's future plans. At least not this afternoon. Tomorrow Erin might ask again, but if she did, hopefully she would approach her dad with the questions instead.

"Then I think we should get it. Maybe one of those too." Leah pointed toward the long purple lacy bed canopy, which attached to the ceiling and draped down around the bed. The color matched the mane of the second unicorn pillow, and as a girl she would've loved to have it in her room.

Erin considered the various colors on display. "I like the green one better."

Since the lime green one did match the third pillow, Leah couldn't steer her toward the purple using that argument. And while it wasn't a color she'd put anywhere in her house, they weren't decorating her bedroom. "Sure. What else do you think we should get?"

A few hours and several shopping bags later, they walked into Gavin's condo. The sound of music greeted them, as well as an aroma Leah couldn't quite put her finger on but that had her mouth watering and her stomach making the most unladylike sounds.

"We're home," Erin called out. "We got everything for my room."

Leah expected her to drop the bags she held and take off, but instead she carried them toward the kitchen, Gavin's most likely location considering the scents filling the air.

Gavin came around the corner and met his daughter before she reached her destination. "Put it all in your room and you can show me later."

"But I want to show you now." Erin's voice came out as more of a whine. It was the first time Leah had heard Erin truly complain about anything Gavin requested of her, but it didn't shock her. Erin was very excited about all the things they'd bought, and she was only nine. Most children didn't like to wait. At least, she'd never liked waiting as a child. She didn't much enjoy waiting now either.

His expression didn't change. Instead he placed a hand on Erin's shoulder. "Dinner is almost done. After we eat, you can show me everything. Promise." Gavin's voice remained calm.

Erin pouted. "Fine." She marched off toward her bedroom, and Leah bit down on her lip to keep from laughing.

Once Erin was no longer within hearing, Gavin spoke again. "Picked up just a few things?" He pointed at the bags Leah held.

"Hey, the room needed a lot of work, and now it'll look like it belongs to a nine- year-old girl instead of a ninety-year-old man."

The beginning of a smile tipped the corners of his mouth as he moved closer. "Thank you for taking her today. I'm sure she had more fun shopping with you than she would've with me."

He stood so close she could feel the heat from his body,

and memories of how he'd woken her this morning pressed forward, causing a shiver of wanting to race through her. Stretching up, she zeroed in on his mouth.

"Anytime," she said before brushing her lips against his, a silent promise of what to expect later tonight when Erin was asleep.

"I'm starving," Erin said, announcing her return. The annoyance at not getting her way was gone and again she sounded like the pleasant young girl Leah had spent the day with.

When they left this morning, Leah had assumed he'd spend the day working since he had the condo to himself. He hadn't. Or at least he hadn't spent it working in his office. The meal set before them had certainly taken some time and effort.

"This must have taken you all day." She eyed the meat on the plate he'd placed in front of her. She wasn't 100 percent certain, but she thought it was lamb.

Gavin set an identical plate, except for the portion size, down in front of Erin. "I wanted something special for my two ladies tonight."

"It smells amazing. What is it?"

Please don't be lamb. She'd tried it on previous occasions and wasn't a big fan. If it was, she'd eat it tonight and smile. Then at some point in the near future, she'd tell him she didn't like lamb so he wouldn't cook it for her again.

He opened his napkin and placed it on his lap then picked up his fork. "Rosemary roasted lamb with haricot mash."

Rosemary, that's what I smell. "What's haricot mash?" It sounded like something fed to farm animals.

"Haricot is a bean. And I mashed it similar to the way you mash potatoes, with olive oil, rosemary, and garlic," he explained.

Beans were another food not near the top of her favorite list.

Across the table, Erin was already eating. Obviously she liked the taste of lamb and didn't mind beans.

Just bite and chew, Leah told herself. Picking up her fork and knife, she prepared to follow her own advice.

"Is there any dessert?" Erin asked between bites.

Leah hoped there was because she wasn't sure how much of this dinner she'd get down.

"Cream buns."

Now those sound delicious.

Leah put the first forkful of meat in her mouth, expecting the flavor she'd come to associate with lamb dishes. She got something much different and wholly delicious.

IN THE BACK of her mind, she'd known for a long time she wanted children someday. Exactly when, she'd never known, but she saw them in her future. Since she'd never been able to envision any of the previous men she dated as fathers, she'd never wasted too much time on the idea.

She didn't need to imagine Gavin as a father. She'd seen him in the role firsthand over the past few days. And he rocked it. Even so, the idea of having children hadn't popped up once until this evening.

Or maybe it had started this afternoon, when Erin asked about her and Gavin having a baby someday. Leah couldn't say for certain.

She did know that helping Gavin tuck Erin in and watching the two of them interact had flipped a switch in her head and heart. She could picture Gavin holding a baby boy with dark hair and dark eyes while she held his twin sister, who oddly enough had blonde hair and Sherbrooke blue eyes.

You're getting a little ahead of yourself.

The reminder didn't help. The image in her head didn't disappear.

"Here you go." Gavin handed her a whiskey sour and joined her on the sofa, a glass of scotch in his hand.

Leah gave herself a mental shake, hoping to dislodge the oh-so-lovely vision. "Erin all set?" He'd no sooner gotten up to make them drinks than Erin had called him down to her room.

"Yep. She couldn't find Sam Sam. I don't know how it got there, but it was under the bed." He sipped his drink and put an arm around her, pulling her in close.

The girl had so many stuffed animals in bed with her, Leah didn't know how she'd noticed one was even missing. "Which one is Sam Sam?"

"The doll in the yellow pajamas with the letters stitched on the chest. Vivian bought it for Erin when she was about nine months old. She's slept with it ever since."

"When is Vivian arriving?"

His fingertips traced circles against her skin in a gentle caress she could sit and experience all night. "Next Wednesday."

They fell into a comfortable silence, enjoying each other's company and their drinks. Unfortunately, Erin's question and the vision of Gavin holding a baby kept creeping back up.

"Did Erin tell you Amber is pregnant?" Leah asked him, rather than the question really in her head, which was *do you want more kids*. Just because Gavin was a great dad didn't mean he saw more children in his future.

He raised his glass toward his lips. "She mentioned it on Saturday. She seems excited about it but hopes the baby is a girl. And I'm happy for Amber. She comes from a big family and always wanted a lot of kids."

Leah wondered if Erin had dropped the same question on him that she'd popped on her.

Only one way to find out. "She asked me if we're going to have a baby too."

He'd just taken a sip of his drink when she shared the statement, and he choked.

Nope, Erin hadn't asked her father the same question.

It took him several seconds to stop coughing. "She what?" he croaked.

"You heard me correctly. She even suggested maybe we could have twins like you and Vivian."

All Erin's stuffed animals could suddenly come to life and stroll out of the room in a conga line and Gavin wouldn't look any more surprised than he did now. Leah suspected she'd worn a similar expression this afternoon while having the conversation in question.

"What did you say?" He no longer sounded like a frog at least, but he didn't sound like himself either.

"I changed the subject and thankfully she didn't ask again."

"Lucky you. She usually doesn't give up until she gets an answer. And usually it has to be an answer she likes."

Yep, she considered herself very fortunate that Erin forgot the matter, or at least never brought it up again.

"What would've been your answer?" Leah hadn't intended to ask him, but now that she had, she decided to go for broke. "Do you even want more kids?"

"I'm not sure about twins, one baby is difficult enough." The laughter in his eyes faded and honesty like she'd never seen replaced it. "But yeah, someday I'd like more. What about you?"

He touched her face; the sensual brush of his fingers over her skin momentarily kept any words from traveling from her brain to her lips. And she knew their relationship was taking a huge leap forward into territory she'd never ventured into before now.

"Definitely."

EVEN WITH THE BLINDS CLOSED, the room exploded with light. A boom followed almost immediately afterward. Turning onto his side, Gavin went to wake Leah. She loved storms and would enjoy the one pressing down around them. He stopped his hand before it reached her shoulder and went back to staring at the ceiling, an activity he'd been engaged in since Leah drifted off to sleep well over an hour ago.

Instead of joining her in dreamland, their conversation kept him awake. Erin's first night here she'd asked if he and Leah were going to get married. Since Amber and Todd were getting married, he'd understood where the question came from. After she informed him Amber was pregnant, he should've anticipated she'd ask if he and Leah were going to have a baby too. He hadn't. And although Leah had managed to get her talking about something else this afternoon, it didn't mean Erin had forgotten about the question. She tended not to forget much. Tomorrow there was a very good chance she'd bring the topic up again; only this time she'd be asking him the question because Leah would be at work.

No matter the situation or question, he told Erin the truth. He would do the same tomorrow.

The storm outside lit up the room again, and Gavin looked at the woman sleeping next to him. He hadn't given her a ring, and they hadn't exchanged any vows, but he couldn't imagine not having her right next to him for the rest of his life. He could honestly say he'd never felt that way about anyone, not even Amber. He'd cared deeply about Amber, but he never saw himself married to her. Even when they'd lived together, he'd asked her to move in with him more because they'd learned she was pregnant than because he wanted to spend his life with her.

And as much as he loved Erin, he hadn't planned on having a child with Amber. It had simply happened.

Erin's innocent question had him thinking about the future and topics that rarely entered his mind. No question about it, he not only wanted Leah in his life forever, but he also wanted children with her someday.

Another clap of thunder exploded, and the warm body pressed against his side moved. Leah's eyes opened and met his as lightning lit up the room again.

"Wow, that was loud," she said, her voice laced with sleep.

He brushed her hair back over her shoulder. "I'm surprised some of the other ones didn't wake you."

"I can usually sleep through anything. Did the storm wake you?" Leah put an arm around his waist and rested her head on his shoulder.

"No, I was still up."

The weight on his shoulder disappeared and Leah propped herself up on one elbow. "Something wrong?"

"Just thinking about tomorrow." *And you.* "Erin didn't bring it up tonight, but now that the question is in her head, there's a decent chance she'll realize you never answered her today. When she does, she'll ask me instead."

"Honestly, I'd rather have her ask you than me."

For the moment the room was again dark so he couldn't see her face, but it sounded like she was smiling.

"Are you going to answer or try to change the subject?" she asked.

"I'll answer because she'll keep asking."

Then he'd ask her a question of his own. After seeing them together, he expected she'd be happy about Leah becoming her stepmother soon, but he still wanted to ask.

Afterward they'd visit some jewelry stores, because at some point in the very near future he was going to need a ring, and he wanted Erin to be a part of the selection process.

Slowly the storm moved away, and Leah fell back asleep with her head still on his shoulder and an arm across his torso. But even with Leah next to him, Gavin remained awake, staring into the darkness and considering the how and when he should propose once he had a ring in hand. Even if they found the perfect one tomorrow, asking anytime in the next week or so was out. He wanted the moment to be memorable but low-key and, most importantly, private. As much as he adored Erin, he didn't want her around when he asked Leah, which meant whatever he decided on would have to wait until she was back in Providence with her mom.

Eventually Gavin forced his eyes closed and drifted off to sleep. Thoughts of his and Leah's future followed him.

GAVIN SKIPPED breakfast but sat at the counter and drank coffee while Leah ate a bagel slathered with cream cheese. At the moment, they had the kitchen to themselves, but although it was early, at any minute Erin might come running in, eager to first redecorate with the things she and Leah bought yesterday and then go on today's outing.

He'd intended to take her hiking since they missed out on it Monday when Gigi showed up. Now he was reconsidering. He had no idea how long Erin's room would take, and he wanted to do some shopping of his own today, which was something else he didn't know how long would take. Gavin wouldn't settle for any old ring. It needed to suit Leah's personality, so he might be visiting a lot of stores over the next few days.

Gavin was making a mental list of all the jewelry stores

he was familiar with when Leah came back from refilling her coffee and sat down. "If you can get her to wait, I'll help Erin with her room when I get back tonight," she offered.

He'd never hung a curtain in his life. Gavin was confident Leah had never done it either, not that it mattered. Getting Erin to wait until tonight so Leah could help wasn't happening. Even getting her into bed last night without putting her new sheets on first had been difficult. She even told them she'd sleep better with the unicorn sheets on the bed than she would with the gray-and-white striped one on there now.

"We'll manage," he replied. "I know you took yesterday off, but is there any way you can take the seventeenth and eighteenth off?"

He should probably make sure the cabin he wanted to rent was available before he asked, but if it was when he called, he wanted to be able to book it. He'd been renting the small cabin up in Maine for years. He'd even asked the current owners, a married couple in the early sixties, if they were interested in selling. They'd declined but promised to let him know before they contacted a real estate agent, because they would be ready to sell in another two or three years.

Overlooking a lake, the cabin was isolated from everyone. He went there once a year to just get away from the city and life in general. Never had he brought anyone along, not even Erin. Gavin wanted to share it with Leah.

"It shouldn't be a problem. Why? What have you got planned?" she asked.

"Maybe nothing. I'll tell you tonight."

Assuming he found the perfect ring in the next week, the cabin would be a perfect place to propose. Even if he didn't, two nights alone there with Leah would be wonderful.

FOURTEEN

Gavin hated when his visits with Erin came to an end. It was no different this time. Today was their last full day together. Tomorrow he'd bring her back to Amber in Providence, and until Thanksgiving he'd be back to seeing Erin only every other weekend.

Disappointment wasn't the only emotion affecting him this time around. Healthy doses of excitement, nervousness, and something bordering on dread had taken their turns over the last two or three days. Right now dread pressed down on his chest.

Leah insisted she didn't care that Harry would be at Piper's party. While he knew she wouldn't make a scene, his half brother was another story. Often the guy didn't think before he opened his big mouth. Gavin worried he'd say something and create an uncomfortable situation for all of them, but especially Leah. Unfortunately, other than keeping her as far from Harry as possible, there wasn't much he could do today.

"It's a little late for an April Fools' joke," Leah said to the person on the other end of the line.

When the device had rang and she checked the screen, she'd merely said it was her brother, so he didn't know if she was talking to Curt or Brett. He guessed it was Curt but only because since he'd known Leah, Brett had never called her.

Gavin checked the side mirror before switching lanes and listened to Leah's half of the conversation.

"You're serious?"

Whatever information her brother was sharing, Leah was having one hell of a time accepting.

She listened to the caller's reply. "Let me know what I can help with. And I'll come and visit soon." Leah ended the call and returned the cell phone to her purse.

He didn't want to be nosy, but his curiosity got the better of him. "Is everything okay?"

Leah's face scrunched up in confusion, and she scratched her head as if still trying to comprehend what her brother had shared. "Yeah, that was Brett. He's entering the special election for Senator Brown's seat in Washington."

Considering the number of politicians in her family tree, he didn't find the news surprising. But she did.

"When I saw him in June, he didn't say anything about leaving active duty. I can't believe he didn't tell me. And he's never said a word about wanting to go into politics."

He didn't tell his sister everything, but a life change like Brett had made did seem like something you'd share with your siblings. If the guy hadn't, Gavin guessed, Brett had his reasons. "Where did he move to?"

The late Senator Brown was from Massachusetts. If Brett was running in the special election to fill the spot left open by the senator's recent death, he had relocated.

She dropped her hand back in her lap. "North Salem. He bought a house there a few years ago but hasn't spent much time there. It's a cute little town. My cousin Jake's wife is originally from there."

He'd never heard of it, but considering the name, it must be located on the North Shore near Salem, a city probably everyone in the United States was familiar with thanks to the famous Salem Witch trials in the early 1690s.

"Brett wouldn't joke about running for the Senate, so I know he's serious. But I never would've expected it from him. One of my cousins, definitely, but not him. He doesn't need it, but I offered to help out with the campaign."

Having the last name Sherbrooke already gave her brother a leg up over whoever he ran against, and they both knew it.

"Are we almost there?" Erin called from the back seat. Until now she'd spent the ride from the city to his dad's home in Stamford, Connecticut, with her head buried in a book while she listened to music.

Hoping to avoid traffic, he'd avoided the highways as much as possible. While it made for a more enjoyable ride, it also made the trip slightly longer. "About another five minutes."

"Modern contemporary" described the architecture style of the home his dad built eight years ago, and at least from the outside it resembled several of the houses near it. While not Gavin's preferred style, he didn't find anything distasteful about the exterior.

The inside was another matter entirely.

Thanks to Kerry, his dad's fourth wife, ostentatious and gaudy were the only two words in the English language that adequately described the home's interior. Since she was only a year older than him, Gavin couldn't think of the former beauty pageant contestant and model as his stepmother. And while she was sweet and seemed to be a good mother, Kerry decorated homes the same way she dressed: to draw attention.

Piper opened the front door and gave him a quick hug and a hello before turning all her attention to Erin. "I've been waiting for you to get here," she said to Erin, who, although neither girl ever thought about it, was technically her niece. "I have to tell you something." Piper grabbed Erin's hand and pulled her toward the staircase.

He didn't think his half sister could have anything left to tell Erin. Since she'd been with him, Erin had talked to Piper on the phone almost every day. Even when she was in Providence with her mom, they talked a few times a week.

"I bet it's about a boy," Leah commented.

"She won't even be eleven until next week." He didn't know what Piper needed to tell Erin, but it didn't involve a boy.

Leah chuckled softly. "Wait. You'll see I'm right."

Dad and Kerry had been married for almost twelve years. To date it was the longest any of Dad's marriages had lasted. Yet even after twelve years, Gavin found it awkward when he introduced Kerry, a woman young enough to be his father's daughter, as Dad's wife.

Linking their hands, Gavin started toward the back of the house. In the summer, his dad's wife liked to entertain outside around the pool. "Have you ever met Kerry?"

"Nope, but I met your dad once," she replied.

He was about to tell her a little about his father's wife when Kerry opened the glass door and stepped inside.

"Gavin." She moved straight toward them, her large breasts barely contained in her bikini top and a sarong tied low around her waist exposing her flat, well-toned stomach. And even from several yards away he could see the large diamond belly ring sparkling in her navel.

Kerry wrapped her arms around him and kissed him on the mouth. Beside him Leah stiffened, and he wished he'd told her all about Dad's wife last night.

"Piper's been driving me crazy wanting to know when you and Erin would get here," she said, dropping her arms back to her sides.

He didn't need to look. He felt Leah's eyes shooting laser beams his way, demanding some answers. If the roles were reversed and some guy planted one on Leah's lips, he'd be demanding answers too.

"Erin didn't want to get out of bed this morning," he explained before he cleared his throat. "Kerry, this is my girlfriend, Leah."

THIS IS GAVIN'S STEPMOM? She picked her chin up off the floor.

At least half her friends and several of her former boyfriends had stepparents, so she'd met plenty of stepmothers. Never had she been introduced to one who was about her own age and dressed like this for a family party. Or one who kissed her stepson on the lips.

"Piper said you were bringing your girlfriend." Kerry looked her way. "It's nice to meet you." Rather than extend a hand, Kerry hugged her, leaving Leah no other choice but to reciprocate.

"Erin told Piper all about the day she spent shopping with you. From what Piper shared, it sounded like you two had a lot of fun. And now Piper is begging to redecorate her room again. We did it last year around Christmas."

Leah wondered if the girl's bedroom was as over the top as what she'd seen so far of the house.

"Your dad and Gigi are outside. I'm going to get another mimosa. Do either of you want one?"

When they both declined, Kerry sauntered off, reminding Leah of a model strutting up and down the catwalk. She waited until the woman was out of earshot before she spoke. "That's your father's wife?" It was an unnecessary question, but it still slipped out.

Considering Piper's age, it made sense Gavin's stepmother was younger than his father. However, she'd expected to meet a woman maybe ten or twelve years younger than Donald Kincaid, not a woman young enough to be his daughter.

A sound she couldn't label escaped him before Gavin spoke. "Yep. There's a considerable age difference between them. But somehow their relationship works. They've been together twelve years. Their marriage has lasted longer than all of Dad's other ones combined."

Maybe the fourth time's the charm.

They joined Gavin's dad and grandmother outside. At the moment they were the only ones there, but the white tent set up suggested a lot of guests were expected for this afternoon's party. Whether they were all family members or Piper's friends was anyone's guess.

"Before the guests arrive, I'd like to speak with you," Donald said after greetings were exchanged. "Assuming you don't mind of course, Leah." He smiled at her, causing him to look even more like an older version of Gavin. "Business matters. I'm sure you know how that goes."

Oh, she knew all too well. Countless times Dad or one of her uncles had needed to address work-related issues in the middle of parties and family gatherings.

Gavin appeared ready to protest, but she spoke up before he could. "I don't mind. Really."

"We'll keep each other company and get to know each other better," Gigi added. "We didn't get much of a chance to talk when I brought Erin home."

Gavin still looked torn between discussing business and sticking by her side. Finally, he squeezed her hand gently before letting go. "I'll be right back."

She watched the two men walk away already in conversation.

"Excellent, they're gone," Gigi said. "Now I can tell you

all about what a wonderful man my grandson is—not that I need to I'm sure. But he is my favorite grandson, and I'd be remiss in my grandmotherly duties if I didn't make sure you knew just what a great man he is."

Her own grandmother might have a favorite grandchild, Leah really didn't know, but if Grama did, she never let it be known.

Gavin never spoke about any cousins. If Gigi's only two grandsons were Gavin and Harry, it was no big surprise Gavin was her favorite. "How many grandsons do you have?"

Gigi patted the chair next to her. "Five. And I have three granddaughters. Gavin is the oldest of the group," she answered before launching into what was clearly one of her favorite topics.

Leah listened patiently as the older woman sang Gavin's praises. Eventually Piper and Erin found their way outside. When Erin spotted her and Gigi sitting together, she pulled Piper over to them.

"When can we do another cooking lesson?" Erin asked, hugging her great-grandmother.

"I'll check with your dad and see what works," the older woman promised. "Have you introduced Piper to Leah yet?"

They'd met briefly while she was dating Harry, but Leah wasn't sure Piper remembered.

"Piper, this is Leah. She's Dad's girlfriend." Erin took care of the introductions.

"I thought you were Harry's girlfriend?" Piper asked.

Great, she remembers meeting me.

Both Erin and Gigi looked as confused as Piper.

"We, ah, we dated for a little while, but it didn't work out. We weren't a good match." *Talk about the understatement of the century.*

"Piper has a new trampoline. We're going to use it. Do

you want to come?" Erin asked, apparently satisfied with Leah's explanation.

She remembered the exact last time she'd used a trampoline. It had been at her uncle's house. Despite the heat, she and her cousins Courtney and Juliette had started a backflip contest on the trampoline. Her first attempt went fine. Somehow on her second she missed the mark and landed on the ground, breaking her arm in two places. She hadn't stepped foot on a trampoline since. Leah wasn't going to break that record today, even if it would make Erin happy.

"I'm going to pass today. But have fun." *And be careful.* She kept the rest of the sentence to herself.

The girls ran off to another part of the estate, leaving Leah alone with Gavin's grandmother.

Gigi folded her wrinkled hands on the table. "Were you and Harry together long?"

It really was none of the woman's business, but Leah preferred not to be rude either, especially since Gavin held the woman in such high regard. "No. We were only together for about two and a half months. We broke up on April Fools' Day."

And he played one hell of an April fools' joke on me that day.

Gigi's lips formed a tight line, and she twisted the wedding band on her finger. "I love Harry. He's my grandson, but I have no illusions about his behavior. Unfortunately when it comes to relationships, he takes after his father. The stories I could tell you about Donald."

One thing she could say about Gavin's grandmother, she didn't hold anything back. It was both refreshing and a bit embarrassing at the same time, because she really didn't want to think about Donald Kincaid's love life.

"If it didn't work out between the two of you, I'm sure it was because of something Harry did."

How did she respond to that?

Thankfully Gigi didn't give her a chance. "Harry and Gavin are nothing alike."

All a person needed to do was spend an hour with the two men to figure that out. "I know."

Smiling, Gigi placed a hand over hers and gave it an affectionate pat. "Good, because my grandson is crazy about you. The day I picked up Erin, he couldn't stop talking about you."

With that final comment, Gavin's grandmother dropped the matter altogether and instead inquired about Leah's skills in the kitchen. When she admitted they were somewhat lacking, Gigi insisted they must rectify the problem soon, and then started to lay out an educational plan for them to follow in the coming weeks and months.

Leah didn't see how expanding her skills in the kitchen could be a bad thing, but months of cooking lessons seemed a bit excessive.

Finally, Gavin's return forced Gigi to temporarily halt the cooking syllabus she was putting together for Leah. He wasn't alone. Vivian and her date were with him.

The screech reached them before Vivian and Leah finished saying hello.

"Aunt Vivian!" Erin's loud voice followed the screech. Piper's excited greeting came right after Erin's, and both girls joined the group.

Other than his daughter, Gavin didn't talk about his family often. However, he'd mentioned how close Vivian was to both girls despite the distance separating them.

Hugs out of the way, Erin's gaze fell on her aunt's date and her mouth fell open. "You're Jeffrey Moore. You're the goalie for Bay City United. I've seen you play."

The man took Erin's hero worship in stride and answered every question she tossed his way. And, man, did she have a lot. Even when Piper tried to get her to go inside and change so they could go swimming, Erin kept right on asking questions and talking about soccer.

"Harry's finally here," Piper chimed in, interrupting Erin midsentence.

Gavin had warned her he might come today. Since so many of the other guests had already arrived and he'd still not shown up, she'd started to hope it meant he was out of town and not going to make it.

Next to her, Erin waved but didn't move. "Hi, Uncle Harry."

Leah's attention momentarily switched away from her and Vivian's conversation to the small group walking toward them. Harry stood between Kerry and a woman who had to be a sister, or a maybe a first cousin. No one could share such a strong family resemblance and not be closely related. Harry had his arm around the unknown woman as they walked toward them.

Once or twice she'd wondered if Gavin ever got around to telling Harry they were together, but never bothered to ask him. Harry's expression when their eyes met immediately answered the question for her.

FIFTEEN

Gavin hadn't been around this many children since Piper's birthday party the previous year. He'd forgotten how much noise a group of ten- and eleven-year-old girls could make, and it wasn't as if they were trying to be so loud. Heaven help them all if they were. They just seemed unable to keep from screeching and having six different conversations at the same time. The endless conversations with relatives he hadn't seen in months and some he'd rather go another few months without seeing weren't helping his headache either. Add to it the heat and oppressive humidity today, and by the time lunch was served, he was ready to call it a day.

Unfortunately, leaving the party wasn't an option. Erin's time with Piper and the rest of his family was limited, so he didn't want to cut it short on her no matter how lousy he felt.

Even if Erin wasn't with him, he might suck it up and deal so Leah could get to know his family. For better or worse, if she agreed to marry him, his family would become hers too. Considering the fact a few members of his family might scare even battled-hardened men away, Leah was handling the gathering well. Even Harry's arrival hadn't ruffled her feathers.

For perhaps the first time, he wished Harry were as shitty a big brother as he was a boyfriend. In true Harry form, he joined the group as if there was no bad history between any of them.

Leah had responded in kind. She hadn't snubbed him or hinted at their previous relationship. Instead she offered up a hello, asked him how he'd been, and once he answered, she went back to her conversation with Vivian as if having her ex-boyfriend standing there was no big deal.

Soon after, the small group broke apart. Harry and Kerry's sister left together and he hadn't spoken to either again today. Piper and Erin raced off to join Piper's friends, while Vivian went to introduce Jeff to their grandmother. He hadn't spoken with either Vivian or Jeff again until they joined them about twenty minutes ago.

Rubbing his temples, Gavin checked his watch. Almost four o'clock and they hadn't even cut the birthday cake—a huge three-tier work of art he'd spotted in the kitchen—yet.

Seated across from him, Vivian, Leah, and Jeff were talking about something. Lost in his thoughts, he'd stopped paying attention, and no one had tried to pull him into the conversation.

"Are you okay?" Leah asked, momentarily putting a halt to her chat with his sister and Jeff.

He skipped nodding since it would likely cause his head to split down the middle and fall onto the table. "Killer headache. The heat isn't helping. Do you mind if I go inside for a little while?" Other than when they first arrived and Dad pulled him aside, he hadn't left Leah alone all day.

"Somehow I'll survive," Leah promised.

The likelihood of Erin looking for him with so many girls

her age around was slim, but... "If Erin wants me, let her know where I am."

Vivian laughed. "Yeah, I don't see that happening, baby brother. But if she needs you, we'll let her know you're inside."

Vivian's comment made Leah laugh too. At another time he'd offer up a reply, but this afternoon Gavin ignored his sister and left for a cooler, quieter location.

Inside the house, it was not only cool but also silent.

After tracking down three ibuprofens, he grabbed a bottle of iced coffee on his way through the kitchen and entered the game room because he doubted any of Piper's friends would come in wanting to play pool. The room's location along the back hallway also made it easier for Erin to find him if she needed him, although he agreed with Vivian's assessment and didn't expect she would.

The windows allowed in sufficient sunlight, so he didn't bother switching on any of the lights in the room. Twisting off the bottle cap, he took a long swig of the cold beverage and hoped the caffeine would assist the medicine sooner rather than later. It was too nice a day to be sitting inside.

Unlike the other rooms, the décor in here made it clear who used this room. There were no bright colors or contemporary works of art on the walls. Leather furniture and dark wood filled the room, along with a full bar, a nine-foot pool table, and a marble chess set. Gavin made himself comfortable in a chair and closed his eyes.

"Needed a break from the noise too?"

Harry's voice broke through his dream, and Gavin sat up straighter in his chair. Falling asleep hadn't been his intention, but at least his head no longer had a drum line practicing in it.

His half brother dropped into the chair opposite him and

gestured toward the chessboard on the table between them. "Up for a game?"

At a different time, he'd take Harry up on the offer. When it came to playing chess, they were equally matched in skill, but a game could last anywhere from ten minutes to over an hour.

"Not today. I don't want to stay in here too much longer."

With a shrug, Harry picked up his drink and raised it toward his mouth. "I can't stick around long either. I told Sharon I'd be back soon. I just wanted to get away from the noise."

Early in the day, he'd noticed Harry had his arm around Sharon, Kerry's sister, but otherwise nothing during their brief conversation had suggested they were involved with each other.

"What happened to Milan?" Gavin asked.

If Harry was still dating the model, Gavin was going to advise he stay away from Sharon.

"I haven't seen her in a couple of weeks. Last I knew, she was headed to Los Angeles."

Well, at least he wasn't screwing around behind the woman's back. It still didn't mean Harry should get involved with Sharon. Considering the age difference, it was easy to forget, but Sharon was their dad's sister-in-law. She often attended family gatherings. A disastrous relationship between the two could make things uncomfortable in the future.

When they'd been younger, he'd given Harry his opinion on his relationships. He'd stopped a long time ago. Gavin wanted to say something now, but he knew it'd only fall on deaf ears. Harry conducted his life the way he wanted. He didn't care what anyone thought.

"How long have you and Sharon been together?"

Harry tipped several of the pawns on the chessboard on their side. "On and off for about a year."

That wasn't the answer he expected to get.

"Kerry's got one hell of a body even after having a kid, but compared to Sharon, she's your average housewife," Harry continued.

Gavin didn't want to think about his stepmother's body or anything else about her.

"What about you? I didn't expect to see you here with a date, never mind with Leah. Dad was pissed when I couldn't get her to take me back. He accused me of screwing up the opportunity of a lifetime. It seemed unlike him when he let the matter go. Now it makes sense. Dad got you to go after her. I guess I owe you one for getting him off my ass."

They weren't the closest of brothers. Their opposite personalities made it impossible. Harry should know him better than to think he'd date anyone because it would benefit the family, and Gavin got ready to tell Harry where he could shove his theory.

The sound of a throat clearing stopped him.

It took all his willpower to not wrap his hands around his brother's throat, because the individual behind him had likely heard Harry's little speech.

Turning in his seat, Gavin witnessed his worst nightmare: Leah crossing the threshold into the room.

Her face was pale except for two pink blotches on her cheeks. Whether her complexion was the result of what she'd most likely heard or something else, he didn't know. Whatever the cause, she didn't bother with a greeting.

"Erin needs you." She sounded out of breath, as if she'd run into the house looking for him, but there was also an angry edge to her tone. "She hurt her ankle. I think it might be broken."

Gavin jumped out of his seat.

"Good, you found him." Vivian appeared in the doorway,

sounding out of breath as well. "Kerry and Dad are with Erin, but she needs you."

No matter what, Erin came first. Fixing any damage caused by Harry's dumbass comments would have to wait.

Thanks to his dad's height, locating him was always easy. This afternoon was no different, and Gavin sprinted across the lawn. Erin was sitting on the grass with Kerry kneeling on one side of her and his dad standing on the other. His daughter had her hands wrapped around her left ankle and tears streamed down her cheeks. The other adults at the party were keeping the rest of the girls away.

Kneeling, he wiped the tears from Erin's face. "It's okay, Bug. I'm here." Gently he moved her hands for a better look. Until now Erin had never seriously hurt herself. He wasn't sure how she'd react to a trip to the emergency room.

"We need to get this checked out," he said softly, because he didn't want to upset her more. Then he lifted her off the ground and cradled her against his body.

Erin sniffed loudly and wrapped her arms around his neck. "Will you stay with me?"

"Of course, Bug." He glanced in Leah's direction. "We might be a while, do you want to wait here?"

He held his breath as he waited for her response. After the conversation she'd most likely overheard, Gavin wasn't sure she'd stick around and wait for him to come back. The likelihood she'd come with them was even slimmer.

"You and Erin might be at the emergency room for hours. I'll give Leah a ride home," Vivian offered before Leah answered.

Gavin couldn't argue with his sister. "Thanks, Viv." He glanced back at Leah, who was standing as far away from him she as could and still be part of the group around Erin. "I'll call you when we're done."

When he only received a slight nod in response, he took a

step forward. For now he'd have to settle for that and worry about the rest later.

"I want Leah to come with us," Erin said, forcing him to come to a halt. "Please."

No one ever looked more torn than Leah did right then. She closed her eyes momentarily. When she opened them again, she focused on Erin. "Sure."

~

LEAH DIDN'T CARE where she was. All she cared about was not being around Gavin right then. She wanted time alone so she could think and sort out her emotions. When Erin asked her to come along, she couldn't refuse—not for a trip to the emergency room. If Erin had been asking her to tag along to the zoo or the movies, it would've been another story. A trip to the hospital, even if it wasn't a life-threatening injury, was another matter.

Although she wasn't the one suffering from an ankle injury, the visit to the emergency room was an incredibly uncomfortable ordeal. Normally conversation flowed easily between them, even when Erin was in the room.

Not tonight.

Instead they'd both sat holding Erin's hands and pretending like Leah hadn't heard every word Harry said. All the while, the conversation she'd walked in on played over and over in her head.

Like it was now.

They'd left the emergency room almost twenty minutes ago. For the first few minutes of the drive, Erin remained awake, but the snores coming from the back seat indicated the events of the day had finally caught up to her.

Pulling up to a stop sign, Gavin checked his rearview mirror as if to make sure Erin was asleep despite the snoring.

"Leah, did you…?" He trailed off. "How much of our conversation did you hear?" It was the most he'd said to her since she found him with Harry.

"Enough."

Gavin swore, something she didn't remember ever hearing him do, and raked a hand down his face.

Is he upset because the truth is out or because Harry was lying?

She wanted to believe the latter. Unfortunately, at the moment she couldn't. At the same time, she was finding it difficult to believe Gavin would pursue a relationship with her simply because his dad wanted him to.

Without saying another word, Gavin turned onto her street. The original plan had been for them to spend the night at her home in Greenwich, since it was closer to his dad's, rather than return to Gavin's condo in the city. Then in the morning they'd drive Erin back to Providence before heading up to Maine.

After this afternoon, she didn't want Gavin staying with her tonight or maybe ever again.

"I can explain." Gavin followed the driveway down to the garage, and the sensor lights went on.

Leah unclipped her seat belt and twisted in her seat. She needed to see his face, see his reaction to her questions. A person could fake their emotions, but she wanted to see his anyway.

"Leah—" he began, but she cut him off. She'd hear him out, but first she had questions.

"Before you say anything else, I need to make sure I understand something." The conversation she overheard had been pretty clear, but on the off chance she'd misunderstood, she wanted clarification.

After unclipping his seat belt, Gavin turned as well. "Ask me anything you want."

"Harry was with me because your father wanted us together?"

She'd met a lot of power-driven individuals, people who stopped at nothing to get ahead in society or in business. She knew couples who had married because it was advantageous for both parties. Rather than as a romantic endeavor, they viewed marriage as a business contract. However, asking your son to be in a relationship because it was an opportunity of a lifetime put Gavin's dad in a class all his own.

Before he could answer, the snoring in the back seat stopped. "Are we at Leah's?" Erin sounded groggy, and Leah expected that once her head hit a pillow she'd fall right back to sleep.

"Just got here, Bug," Gavin replied, glancing into the back seat.

"Good. I'm tired. I want to go to bed."

Finally, Leah knew what it took to tire his daughter out.

Words weren't necessary. Gavin's expression when he looked back at her asked the question for him. *Do you want us to spend the night?*

No. But it was late, and she didn't know how to explain a sudden change in plans to a nine-year-old girl who'd just left the emergency room with a broken ankle.

"Then we better get you inside," she said. The house had plenty of bedrooms. She'd survive the night with him under her roof.

Although Erin had a pair of crutches, Gavin carried her from the car and into the house. He followed Leah up the staircase to the second floor and down a hallway. Opening the door to the only full guest suite in the home, she switched on the light. Unlike the guest bedroom across the hall that only had a private bathroom, the suite had a full bathroom complete with a Jacuzzi tub *and* a separate sitting area.

"Erin can use this room. If you want to be close, you can

sleep on the sofa in here or you can use the room across the hall."

And I'll be in my room on the opposite side of the house. Alone.

She'd carried their overnight bags inside, since he had his hands full carrying Erin. Leah dropped them on the floor near the door. "Goodnight, Erin. Gavin, I'll be in the kitchen." She didn't stick around for a response from either of them.

She filled the teakettle with water and set it on the stove before selecting a canister of loose leaf tea from the cupboard. She didn't feel like tea, but brewing a pot the proper way, which according to her cousin was the only way to make it, gave her something more productive to do than chew her fingernails while she waited for Gavin. And he would come. Gavin didn't leave conversations unfinished, no matter the topic.

By the time he finally joined her, the tea leaves were steeping in the china teapot Sara had given her as a gift one year ago.

"Sorry. She wanted me to stay with her until she fell asleep." He didn't try to touch her. Instead he pulled out a chair at the table opposite her and sat. "What you heard isn't true," he began before she could ask any other questions.

"Then Harry didn't get involved with me because your father wanted him to? Because it sure sounded like it to me."

"No, not in the beginning. But he stayed with you because Dad wanted him to," Gavin admitted. "I didn't know that until the day you found him with Amy."

He sounded sincere. She'd give him that much.

"And when your dad found out I asked you to Newport, he asked you to take over since Harry blew it with me?"

"Only Vivian knew you invited me along on the Fourth."

That she wasn't buying. "You saw him the morning you came to pick me up."

"Yeah, but I didn't tell him we had plans. Before today, he didn't know you and I were together. I don't discuss any of my relationships with him."

Gavin and his dad worked together. They talked on the phone. How could his father not know? Maybe if they'd only gone on a single date, she could accept his claim. She didn't share the names of every man she dated with her parents. But they'd been together for over a month. Not only that, but lately she'd been spending more nights at his condo than her house. While she hadn't shared those details with her parents —talking about her sex life wasn't something she felt comfortable doing even with Mom—her family knew the relationship was serious between them.

He reached across the table and took her hand. "I'm telling you the truth. I'm with you because I love you, not for any other reason. When Dad saw you with me today, he was as surprised as Harry."

She wanted his words to be true and his feelings to be real. But wanting something to be real didn't make it so. If it did, unicorns would be real because as a little girl she'd always wanted one for a pet.

Tugging her hand free, Leah poured her tea. She didn't offer Gavin a cup. Instead she walked away to get some milk and sugar. If he wanted any, he didn't mention it.

"The day you dumped Harry, I was mad at him for treating you like that. But I was also happy because *I* wanted to be with you," he continued, putting extra emphasis on the word I. "If you hadn't been with someone the first time we met, I would've asked you out then. When you showed up at my condo with Harry, I was pissed because if I'd known you weren't with anyone, I would've tried to contact you before your cousin introduced you to him."

Leah sipped her tea and considered his words. She'd

never heard anyone sound more sincere. But sincerity didn't equate with truth.

"Leah?" His voice cracked with emotion.

Her heart urged her to accept Gavin's words and forget everything she'd heard Harry say this afternoon.

Her brain cautioned her against it. Twice men had betrayed her. She didn't want to add a third to her track record.

"I need some time."

Time to think and sort through everything they'd shared up until today as well as their conversation tonight. Leah couldn't even attempt to do that with him sitting across from her.

He steepled his hands together near his face and closed his eyes. She waited for him to further argue his case or press her for a different answer.

He didn't. Instead he lowered his hands and opened his eyes. They shone with the same sadness gripping her heart. Unfortunately, she couldn't tell if it was real or not.

"Okay. Take whatever time you need." Standing, Gavin came around to the other side of the table. He didn't try to hug her or pull her in close. He simply took her hand and raised it to his lips. "I love you, and time won't change that." His lips brushed across her knuckles before he released her hand. "Goodnight. I'll see you in the morning."

Leah swallowed, trying to dislodge the softball stuck in her throat. "Goodnight." She watched him leave the room and reached for her teacup. Getting any sleep tonight was unlikely. She might as well drink her tea and try to sort out the thousand and one emotions crashing over her.

SIXTEEN

Until about a month ago, unless she had a family member visiting or she was with friends, she spent her weekends at home alone. The solitude never bothered her.

This morning the house was a little too quiet and a little too big.

After a quick breakfast, Gavin and Erin had left as planned for Providence. She expected him to press her for an answer regarding where they stood before he left, but he didn't mention their late-night conversation or the one she'd overheard between him and Harry. Erin did ask why she wasn't coming along when it was time to leave. As far as she knew, Gavin and Leah were going to Maine after they dropped her off today.

Thankfully, a simple "Leah has something she needs to do" from Gavin satisfied Erin, and she let the matter go. Or at least she didn't ask again before they left. What happened once Gavin and Erin got underway was anyone's guess, and not her problem today.

She had enough of her own to sort out.

Last night Gavin had promised her all the time she

wanted, but she didn't want this lingering between them. Either she accepted that he was telling the truth and they moved on, or she told him to take a hike and got on with her life.

Option B was certainly the easiest and perhaps safest. If she put an end to their relationship now, she didn't run the risk of getting burned down the road.

But cutting him from her life was the last thing she wanted. Even after the conversation she'd overheard, she loved him. Maybe that made her an idiot, but she couldn't turn her emotions on and off like a table lamp. Not only did she still love him, but she wanted to believe her feelings were reciprocated.

Unfortunately, even after their conversation, doubt remained, urging her to think long and hard before she got in any deeper. And that was why at almost noon on a picture-perfect Sunday afternoon, she sat alone by the pool sipping iced tea and running through every moment she spent with Gavin since April.

True, he'd called to check on her after the incident at the condo, but he hadn't asked to see her. She'd been the one to reach out a few days later and ask him to lunch. Their friendship had taken off after that afternoon. Not once had she felt as if he was pursuing her or trying to set himself up for something more.

Maybe his dad hadn't asked him to pick up where Harry failed yet. She hated to think like that, but it was certainly a possibility.

Gavin insisted his dad never knew about her invitation to Newport. Maybe that was true. It was also possible he'd found out the morning Gavin picked her up and made his request then. After all, they kissed for the first time on the Fourth. Before then she'd never suspected Gavin's feelings ran any deeper than friendship.

If they had, wouldn't she have seen some signs? A flash of jealousy maybe when they were out and other men spoke to her, or a casual touch when they were golfing or talking? She'd certainly suffered her fair share of jealousy when they'd been together and a woman showed any interest in him.

"Maybe he's good at hiding his emotions."

Some people were. Her eldest brother, Brett, could be falling apart inside and no one would ever know. He could control and mask his emotions better than anyone she knew. Even Curt did a decent job of only letting people see what he wanted them to.

"He's certainly great at keeping secrets," she muttered into her drink before taking a sip. Although they'd spent time together for months, he'd never mentioned Erin. If that wasn't being able to keep one hell of a secret, she didn't know what was.

Last night she hadn't dwelled on the fact he'd only told her about Erin when he absolutely had to. With everything else, it was another strike against him.

Leah rested her forehead against her bent knees. *I'm getting nowhere.*

She was having the same arguments with herself now that she had last night in bed. Maybe a long walk would help clear her head. If not, at least she'd get a change of scenery.

Finishing the last of her iced tea, she stood. At the same moment her cell phone rang.

"Are you up for company? I'm about five minutes from your house," Curt asked after she answered.

Some company might be the perfect distraction this afternoon. "Definitely."

She expected both Curt and Taylor, perhaps even Reese, to be on the other side of the door when she opened it, but only her bother stood on the step.

"How's my favorite sister?" Curt asked, hugging her and dropping a kiss on her cheek.

"I'm your only sister," she replied, returning the embrace.

Pulling away, Curt ruffled her hair as if she was Reese's age and smiled. "Doesn't mean you're not my favorite."

"If you're looking for me to return the sentiment, it's not happening. And you know it." Leah loved her brothers equally. Although they were different in most ways, they'd both always been fabulous older brothers, and she'd never claimed to favor one over the other.

"That's okay. I know the truth, and I promise not to tell Brett. We wouldn't want to hurt his feelings."

Yep, some teasing from her brother was just the thing she needed this afternoon. "All alone today?" she asked. From what she'd seen and been told by other family members, Curt and Taylor rarely spent their free time apart.

"Yeah. I spent the night at Scott's. We went to see the New York/Boston game last night. Taylor couldn't make it. She had a bridal shower to go to yesterday. Someone she went to college with." He looked around before he continued. "Gavin's not here?"

Leah shook her head. "He's driving Erin back to Providence. Let's go sit outside. It's too nice to stay in here."

He waited until they were seated near the pool before speaking again. "I'm surprised you didn't go with him. Did things not go well between you and Erin?"

Reaching out, she adjusted the umbrella so they were both in the shade. "We got along great. I didn't want to go with them today."

"I told you, you had nothing to worry about." He took his sunglass off his head and set them on the table. "Since Erin won't be around next weekend, why don't the two of you come and visit. I completed what used to be the ballroom."

He'd extended the same invitation before Erin's arrival.

He'd even suggested they bring her along. Then she'd declined because of all the activities Gavin already had planned with Erin. Today she really wished she could accept… but at the moment she couldn't.

Leah adjusted her position so she faced forward rather than her brother. "Maybe I'll come up. I'll let you know before Friday." Ready for a new topic altogether, she asked, "Did you hear Brett's news?"

Unfortunately, Curt didn't take the bait. "It seemed odd you didn't go with Gavin to Providence, but if you're trying to change the subject, I know something's up. What happened?"

Over the years, she'd gone to her brother for advice regarding work and even school. Never once had Leah sought him out for advice regarding her romantic relationships. When she needed that, she called Tory or Allison, occasionally even Courtney, but Curt was a good listener. More important, he was here and her cousins weren't. If she explained the situation, he might be able to help her sort through things. Either that or he might offer to beat Gavin up for her.

"Yesterday we went to a party and I overheard a conversation between Harry and Gavin. I wasn't trying to eavesdrop. I was looking for him because Erin hurt herself and needed him. But the how I heard doesn't matter. Harry thinks their father encouraged Gavin to get involved with me after I wouldn't take him back. Turns out Harry stayed with me because their father wanted the connections."

Curt crossed his arms and digested the words. "From what I know about Harry, it doesn't surprise me. I never understood why you dated him, and I expected you to kick his ass to the curb long before you did. The same goes for their father. Using his son's relationships to benefit himself or the company sounds like something he'd try. And we both know he wouldn't be the first person to do it. "

How she should've handled her previous relationship was irrelevant at this point. Only her current one mattered. "Anyway, when I confronted Gavin, he denied it. But I'm not sure I should believe him."

"You've spent more time with him than me, but I don't see him doing something like that. He seems like a decent guy. And I'm not the only one who says that about him."

"What, do you conduct background investigations on the men I date or something?" Curt played the role of a typical protective big brother from time to time, but he'd never hinted at digging around to learn more about the men she got involved with.

"No, but considering his father and brother's—"

"Half brother," she clarified.

Curt glared at her, and for the first time all day she cracked a smile. Regardless of age or the situation, sometimes it was simply fun to annoy one's older brother.

"Considering their reputations and what Harry did when you were together, I was concerned about you. Gavin and I have some of the same friends and acquaintances, including his stepbrother, Evan, so I reached out to a couple."

Should she hug him for being so concerned or slap him for butting his nose in where it didn't belong? Maybe both.

"None of them found it weird?" she inquired.

"Not the way I asked. And you can do what you want, but unless Gavin has lied to you in the past or given you another reason not to trust him, I'd give him the benefit of the doubt on this one. Forget what Harry said and move on."

"He waited until I confronted him before he told me about Erin," she pointed out.

"Withholding info is not the same as lying."

"Gee, thanks, Professor Sherbrooke. I didn't know that."

Curt ignored her sarcastic reply. "Hey, I agree with you. He shouldn't have waited to tell you about his daughter, but maybe he had his reasons. I did something similar in the spring. Only Trent and Gray know, but when I met Taylor and her family, they didn't know who I really was."

She couldn't help herself. "And who did they think you were, Santa Claus?"

If looks could injure you, she'd be suffering big time right then.

"Curt S. Hilton, the author. My point is, he's not the first person to not share personal information until they're ready. And since he came clean as soon as you confronted him, I wouldn't hold it against him. Just like I wouldn't hold Harry's action against Gavin."

Curt had no reason to fabricate such a story; still she found it hard to accept. And in her opinion, what he'd done was far worse than Gavin simply withholding information, because while C. S. Hilton was Curt's pen name, he'd lied to Taylor and her family.

"They didn't recognize you?"

"Nope, not until I shaved off the beard, cut my hair, and ditched the glasses," he explained.

She tried to envision her clean-shaven brother with a beard and long hair but couldn't do it. "You're lucky Taylor forgave you. I'm not sure I would've."

They both fell silent. Leah didn't know what was occupying her brother's thoughts, but everything Curt had said since she opened up to him was going through her head.

"One last thing and I'll drop it. Taylor's an excellent judge of character, probably because of her job. And she liked Gavin," Curt explained. Then true to his word, he changed the subject. "Brett's running for a seat in the Senate. I'm not sure what to think. I can't picture him in Washington. Can you?"

No, but their elder brother wouldn't be the first male Sherbrooke to surprise her. "A few years ago, I never would've pictured either Jake or Trent married with children either."

ERIN'S COMPANY and conversation kept him engaged throughout the ride from Connecticut to Rhode Island, so keeping thoughts of Leah at bay had been manageable. Unfortunately, an empty condo didn't do the same.

After dropping Erin off and offering Amber and Todd his congratulations on their baby news, he debated on whether to drive back to New York or crash at his apartment in Providence. In the end, he'd opted to hop back on the highway and head home. If on the off chance Leah called and asked him over, he didn't want to be hours away.

Not that he expected her to call tonight or even tomorrow.

At least tomorrow he'd have work to distract him. Since they wouldn't be in Maine as planned, taking the day off was pointless.

Usually he'd be thankful for a drive without any traffic. Tonight he would've welcomed it, because even light traffic would've given him something other than his and Leah's relationship to focus on. Instead he made the entire trip back to New York without hitting a single trouble spot until he reached the city.

When he opened the door, a dark empty room greeted him. The place always seemed emptier than normal somehow after Erin's visits, and it often took a couple days to return to normal. Tonight the feeling was a thousand times worse. A couple days wasn't going to change it either. He'd grown too accustomed to coming home to Leah almost every night for the emptiness to seem normal anytime soon.

Even with all the travel he did, Gavin never left a bag packed. No matter the time when he got home from any kind of trip, he made a point of emptying out his suitcase or overnight bag right away. Now he left the bag he'd packed for their getaway on his bedroom floor and only removed the diamond ring he and Erin had picked out.

Flipping up the cover, he looked at it. Instead of sitting inside a box, it should be on Leah's finger. Thanks to Harry, that might never happen. Opening his mouth and suggesting their father asked him to get involved with Leah was one thing. Doing it in a place where anyone could walk in and overhear the conversation was another.

He'd never loved Harry the same way he did Vivian or even Piper. Since Harry's mother had been the other woman when his parents were married, it was understandable. Especially since Mom filed for divorce when she learned that not only was Dad cheating on her but he had another baby on the way. At least it was understandable in Gavin's eyes. Still, he'd never disliked Harry.

All that changed yesterday.

Now his emotions toward the guy bordered on hate.

Gavin closed the ring box, shoved it in a drawer, and hoped the old adage "out of sight, out of mind" would work this evening.

He'd promised her all the time she needed. Gavin intended to honor his promise, which meant calling her less than twenty-four hours after uttering those words was not an option.

But damn, he wanted to hear her voice.

Tell her he loved her.

Hear her say the same back to him.

"Not happening tonight."

Watching and waiting for the phone to ring accomplished nothing useful, so Gavin left his cell on his nightstand and retreated to his office. Work had always filled his days and nights before, but he'd never needed it to do that more than he did this evening.

If work didn't distract him, there was always the kitchen. Although he didn't often have the time to do it, he found cooking almost as therapeutic as physical activity. A few hours experimenting with some recipes had an added bonus exercise didn't: he'd have some food ready to eat in his refrigerator this week.

~

"HELLO."

The knife almost missed the onion on the cutting board and landed on his finger instead.

Onions might make a person cry, but not hear voices. If Leah was here, she'd made her decision.

Please let it be the decision I want.

Grabbing a towel, Gavin wiped his hands and checked the time on his watch. Almost ten o'clock already? He'd been working longer than he'd realized. Unable to get anything useful accomplished in his office, he'd given up around six and made a trip to the grocery store for ingredients. He'd been cooking ever since.

Gavin tossed the towel aside and lowered the flame beneath the pot on the stove. "I'm—"

"Cooking," she said, entering the kitchen. "And whatever you're making smells amazing." She stopped behind one of the stools near the counter.

"Just playing around. I needed something other than work to focus on when I got back from dropping off Erin," he admitted.

He didn't care if it made him sound pathetic or not. It was the truth. No matter how hard he tried to focus, his mind had kept replaying the afternoon they'd made love in his office.

She gripped the back of the barstool and moistened her lips. "I sent you a text before I came, but when you didn't answer, I assumed you were still on the road. I planned to wait if you weren't here when I arrived."

"No, I've been home for a while. I left the phone in my bedroom, and I haven't checked it since. Sorry about that, but I'm glad you came." He moved in her direction, intent on pulling her close and not letting go again until tomorrow.

Common sense kicked in before he reached her. Just because she stood in his kitchen didn't mean she was about to give him the news he wanted to hear. Some people preferred to deliver both pleasant and unpleasant news in person.

"Last night you told me to take all the time I needed," Leah began, getting right to the point. "I don't need any more time, Gavin. I don't know about you, but last night I couldn't sleep because I was thinking about us and about what Harry said. I did the same all day today."

Is she intentionally stalling or is it me?

"When I found Harry here with Amy, it made me angry. Not because I loved him but because he betrayed my trust. But it didn't hurt. When he suggested you were only with me because of your father, it was like he'd dropped a granite boulder on me. Honestly, I couldn't think past the pain or the idea that, if it was true, you'd betrayed me too."

He got the pain part. When he'd seen her in the doorway, it'd been like a bomb exploded in his chest.

"I think your dad is a jerk for asking Harry to stay with me because it'd give him some connections." She paused and shook her head. "No, jerk is too mild a word. He's worse, and so is Harry for agreeing. But I was wrong yesterday. I should've known better. You've never given me any reason to doubt you. And I know you're nothing like Harry or your dad. I realized that back in the winter, and I should've reminded myself of it yesterday, but the shock overwhelmed me. And I know even if your father asked you to do something like Harry described, you wouldn't agree."

His feet moved again. This time they didn't stop until he rounded the kitchen counter and stood an arm's length away. "When it comes to my father and his behavior, trust me, it's better I don't give you my opinion. But you're right, if he'd asked me the same thing he did Harry, I wouldn't have agreed. But believe me when I tell you he didn't. The only reason I want to be with you is because I love you."

His mind and body found it unacceptable to be this close and not have her in his arms. Gavin closed the gap between them, and his arms instinctively wrapped around her waist. "I love you," he repeated, because saying it once wasn't enough.

She parted her lips to speak. Gavin hoped she intended to tell him the same, but either way she'd have to wait. Leah wasn't pushing him away, and all day he'd wondered if he'd ever get a chance to kiss her again. With her in his arms, he planned to do it now.

Even though he wanted to pick her up and carry her down the hall, Gavin forced himself to keep the kiss tender and closemouthed. Right now he needed it to communicate his love, not his desire.

THEY'D SHARED everything from sweet kisses to passionate ones and everything in between. This one, though, melted her soul. Told her without words what was in his heart.

When he pulled his lips away, she cupped his face in her hands. "I love you too." She gave him a peck on the lips. "And I think whatever is in the oven is burning."

When she'd walked in, the smell of meat cooking and spices had filled the air. Now it contained a hint of smoke as well. She wasn't an expert in the kitchen, but she knew smoke wasn't a good sign.

He let go as if she was the one on fire instead of the oven's contents. "Damn it."

Gavin opened the door, and as a billow of smoke poured into the kitchen, he immediately switched on the exhaust fan over the stove.

He set down a pain holding the charred remains of something it might take a forensic scientist to identify.

"I know you said you were experimenting, but I hope this dish isn't intended for any of Culloden's restaurants because I don't think it'll be a customer favorite." She moved closer in case a better look might help her identify the blackened mass. It didn't help.

"It was supposed to be edible, right?" she asked trying not to laugh.

"Started off as venison cottage pie. There's no hope of salvaging any of it." He turned off the flame under a pot and moved it to the back of the stove. "I was working on making some soup too."

Coming up behind him, she wrapped her arms around his waist and pressed her body into his. "It's okay. I'm not hungry." She stretched up and kissed the back of his neck. "How about I help you clean up this mess up and then we go to bed." Leah left a trail of kisses along his neck and to his ear.

"I've got a better idea. We go to bed now, and I'll deal with this tomorrow."

She released the button on his shorts and then slipped a hand inside to touch him. "Your idea sounds much better."

EPILOGUE

New Year's Eve

BACK IN JULY when Leah had invited him to the annual Sherbrooke New Year's Eve party at Cliff House, Gavin never imagined he'd be asking her to marry him. It was his plan for this evening.

Several times since August he'd considered proposing, yet somehow the timing never seemed quite right. Tonight he was done waiting.

With Leah still in the bathroom applying makeup, he pulled the jewelry box out of his suitcase and slipped it inside his tuxedo jacket.

"I'm almost ready," she called to him through the closed door.

She'd said the same thing half an hour ago, so it was anyone's guess how much longer before she was done. Any other night he wouldn't care how long she took getting ready, but each second that passed right now equaled a lifetime. He had no reason to doubt she'd accept his proposal. Regardless, until he heard the words and slipped the ring on her finger, the knots in his stomach weren't going anywhere.

His fingers brushed across the box in his pocket. "No rush. I'll be in the other room." What else could he say? Get your butt out here now so I can ask you to be my wife? Not exactly the most romantic proposal ever.

Gavin opened the suite's sliding glass door and stepped out on their hotel balcony. Although they'd been invited to stay with several of her relatives in Newport, including her parents, they'd decided to book a hotel suite instead. Already the temperature outside was cold, and it would only get colder as the evening wore on. It didn't faze him. Actually, it was just the opposite. He felt his body relaxing. The knots in his stomach loosened and the tension he hadn't even realized he had in his shoulders started to melt away as he listened to the waves.

"Aren't you freezing out there, Gavin?"

His stomach clenched back up. *She'll say yes*, he reminded himself before he turned around.

"No, I—" Whatever else he intended to say made a mad dash out of his head when he caught sight of Leah. He'd seen her dressed elegantly on other occasions, most recently the night her brother won the election, but nothing prepared him for the vision standing before him. "You look incredible," he managed once he found his voice again.

"And you look cold. You're going to freeze to death out there." She moved closer to the door but didn't actually come outside.

With her standing there looking like that, there was no chance of it happening. "I'm fine." He stepped back inside and closed the slider behind him. Gavin pulled at the tie suddenly making it difficult to breathe while his other hand clenched around the box in his pocket.

"It just started and I'm done with winter. When Erin

comes to stay with us for February break, we should take her someplace warm instead of skiing," she said.

Although he still had his condo in the city for the nights they both worked late or simply didn't feel like fighting traffic, Gavin had officially moved into her home in Connecticut in September. And like Leah had during the summer, she helped Erin redecorate the bedroom she used when with him.

"If you can convince her to skip a week of skiing, I'll change our reservations for a hotel on the beach in the Bahamas."

Leah put her arms over his shoulders and smiled. "Consider it done."

Erin loved skiing almost as much as he did. Getting her to change her mind would take considerable effort. But if anyone could do it, Leah could. An amazing relationship existed between Leah and Erin. Occasionally he even felt a little left out on the weekends they were together. And although she'd never come out and said it, Gavin knew Erin considered Leah to be another mom.

Releasing his death grip on the box, Gavin pulled his hand from his pocket. "I know you want to leave." He placed his palms on her waist as he spoke. "But—" A strong knock echoed through the hotel suite. "Expecting someone?" he asked, because he certainly wasn't.

"You could say that."

Confused, he watched her walk away.

WHEN IT CAME TO PROPOSING, the man bought the ring and did the asking. At least that was what books and movies wanted you to believe. Maybe it was true for most couples. It didn't work for Leah. This was the twenty-first century, and honestly she was tired of waiting for Gavin to get around to asking. She knew he planned to eventually; thanks to Erin she knew he had a ring. Two weeks after Piper's birthday party, she'd gone with Gavin to Providence for his weekend with Erin. While Gavin was out picking up pizzas, Erin asked if she wasn't wearing the beautiful diamond ring Gavin bought her because she didn't like it. She then went on to share how they'd gone to a ton of stores and that Gavin let her help pick it out so she really hoped Leah liked it.

Ever since, she'd been waiting for Gavin to pull the ring out. Almost four months of waiting was long enough. The time had come for her to take things into her own hands.

She signed the receipt and handed the portfolio back to the gentleman after he set the tray down and opened the wine bottle for them. "Thank you," she said, following him to the door and closing it behind him.

Until this very moment, the idea of proposing hadn't bothered her. Crossing back toward him, her hands shook so much she worried the wine would spill out.

When she reached him, she didn't hand him a glass. Instead she set them on the nearby end table and tried to unglue her tongue from the top of her mouth.

Gavin's gaze darted to the drinks and then back at her, wearing perhaps the most adorably confused expression she'd ever seen.

"Gavin," she began.

He opened his mouth to speak, but she placed a finger against his lips.

"Gavin," she repeated, suddenly feeling sympathetic for her brothers, who'd both proposed to their girlfriends earlier in the month. "Will you marry me?"

She'd spent the week picturing this moment in her head. She'd envisioned him kissing her, or saying yes and then kissing her. He did neither.

He laughed.

"You're not supposed to laugh."

Pulling a box from his pocket, he opened it. “Before we got interrupted, I was about to ask you the same thing.” He plucked the ring out and tossed the empty box on the table.

Taking her hand, Gavin slipped the ring on her finger and then kissed her. “Yes, I will marry you. I can’t imagine spending my life with anyone else. You’re my perfect partner and a wonderful mother to my daughter. I love you.”

She glanced down at the ring on her finger. Erin and Gavin definitely had good taste in jewelry. “Erin was right. It is beautiful.” Leah handed him a wineglass.

“She told you about it? When?”

“In August. She wanted to know why I wasn’t wearing it.”

Gavin appeared a little shell-shocked as he set the glass down. “You never even hinted you knew about it.”

“Oh, believe me, I wanted to, but I assumed you would ask when you were ready. But I got sick of waiting. And so you know, I want a short engagement.”

“Whatever you want,” he agreed.

She hoped he’d say that. “How does Valentine’s Day sound?” Corny or not, she’d always thought a wedding on Valentine’s Day would be romantic.

“You want to get married in seven weeks?”

“I already checked the dates. Erin will be with us that weekend anyway, and I know Uncle Mark will perform the ceremony.”

He touched his glass to hers. “Then Valentine’s Day it is.”

The End.

OTHER BOOKS BY CHRISTINA

The Sherbrookes of Newport

Loving The Billionaire

The Teacher's Billionaire

The Billionaire Playboy

The Billionaire Princess

The Billionaire's Best Friend

Redeeming The Billionaire

More Than A Billionaire

Protecting The Billionaire

Bidding On The Billionaire

Falling For The Billionaire

The Billionaire Next Door

The Billionaire's Homecoming

Love On The North Shore

The Courage To Love

Hometown Love

The Playboy Next Door

In His Kiss

A Promise To Keep

Elite Force Security

Born To Protect

Made in United States
North Haven, CT
20 October 2021

10468163R00135